"C'mon, my little fantasy. Give me something to take back with me."

Relenting, Stevie stood, and, slower this time, pulled her shirt free and relieved the final two buttons. She stopped long enough to toss her cap onto the bed.

Jade was wound for sound, hooting, whistling, and clapping rhythmically as Stevie playfully tossed the shirt to her. "All of it! Take it all off!"

Jade gasped pleasurably at the sight of Stevie's small firm breasts and muscular shoulders. Too shy to dance, Stevie toyed with the zipper of her pants, triceps bulging.

About the Author

Tracey Richardson was born and raised near Windsor, Ontario. She now makes her home in Central Ontario's Georgian Bay area with her partner, Sandra, and their retrievers, Cleo and Rollie. Tracey is a journalist at a daily newspaper, and when not working or writing, likes to tool around in her classic Corvette. Her previous novels, all published by Naiad Press, include *Last Rites* (1997) and *Northern Blue* (1996). She has also contributed short stories to *Dancing in the Dark* and *Lady Be Good*.

2nd Stevie Houston Mystery

Over the Line

TRACEY RICHARDSON

THE NAIAD PRESS, INC.
1998

Printed in the United States of America on acid-free paper
First Edition

Editor: Lila Empson
Cover designer: Bonnie Liss (Phoenix Graphics)
Typesetter: Sandi Stancil

Library of Congress Cataloging-in-Publication Data

Richardson, Tracey
    Over the line / by Tracey Richardson.
       p.   cm. — (Stevie Houston mystery : 2nd)
    ISBN 1-56280-202-X (alk. paper)
    I. Title.   II. Series: Richardson, Tracey, 1964–   Stevie
Houston mystery ; 2nd.
PS3568.I3195O94   1998
813'.54—dc21   97-52740
                                                 CIP

To Sandra —
first, last, always

Acknowledgments

Thanks to my partner, Sandra Green, for her love and support. She is my Top Cop! I have been fortunate to have Brenda's support and expertise for not only the technical forensic references in this novel, but for her overall critical eye as well, so thank you, Brenda F. My gratitude to my friends (you all know who you are) and family for their support. Thank you to my editor, Lila Empson, Naiad Press, and the staff of Naiad.

PROLOGUE

The streets, like a sleeping giant, were still lifeless at this early hour. But that wouldn't last long, Harding Scott knew.

Any minute now, the giant would stir, rumble, and groan, taking on a clumsy, cacophonous life all its own. Cars and people, like adrenaline-infused blood, would soon pump furiously through the capillaries of Toronto. The thunder of streetcars and underground subways would rattle the pavement, the shrill of horns and sirens would split the air, and the muffled clusters of conversations would remind Scott there was more to this city than steel and concrete.

This was his favorite time of day, and the only way he could tolerate a visit to Toronto — this gentle easing into it. His own much smaller, border-straddling city, Shelton, was two hours behind him now. And since his semiannual checkup with his cardiologist wasn't until later in the morning, he looked forward to a leisurely breakfast with the *Globe & Mail*, and a good dose of people watching.

He touched the glass of the car's side window. *Still cold out.* A little shiver shot through him. He frowned at the snowbanks, illuminated blue by the ubiquitous streetlights. The bulbs cast perverse shadows, managing to make one of the city's few natural components look grotesquely artificial.

Headlights, those same square headlights he'd already seen three times this morning, loomed in his rearview mirror again, growing fatter, blindingly bathing the inside of his car.

Goddammit, get off my ass! He slowed, then sped up, neither maneuver shedding the irritating car behind. Finally, he pulled over to let it pass. Strangely, he felt relieved when it swung around him, and he squinted hard at the passing license plate, as only a cop would do.

Abruptly, the car pulled in front of him, cut his path diagonally, and squealed to a stop. *What the hell is this?* Scott's hand brushed the gearshift, his foot ready on the clutch. As the two men strode briskly from the car toward him, his heart, his weak-assed sonofabitch-of-a-heart, began to tremble erratically like a bowl of Jell-O.

Scott knew a takedown when he saw one. He knew

what this was, all right. He jammed the gearshift into reverse, released the clutch. But his nervous foot was too quick. The car stalled. *Fuck!* His throat burned, and his heart — was it even beating anymore? — jammed his throat too.

Both doors were yanked open, almost off their hinges.

"What the fuck do you want?" Scott shrieked in a voice like a little girl's.

The big one with the brush cut and the square jaw smiled, teeth bleached and perfectly aligned like the slats of a fence, dark glasses hiding what were surely evil eyes. Scott had seen that face before, but where? Back home in Shelton, somewhere . . .

"Here, take my wallet, my keys —"

A slap stung his face, flooded his eyes. Big gloved hands, brutal and impatient, pulled him from the car while the other man, who had already snatched the keys from the ignition, opened the trunk, a semiautomatic pistol in his other hand.

"Get the fuck in."

It was all Harding Scott would ever hear again. And as the trunk closed and darkness shrouded him, he knew there would be no mercy, no goodbyes.

He felt surprisingly calm, wondered if that was normal. He felt detached from himself, and his cop's mind buzzed with morbid curiosity as he felt the car move beneath him. How would they kill him? Would they beat him to death? Maybe slash his throat? Shoot him?

The air in the cramped trunk — what little of it there was — was thick and hot and smelled of his own sweat, his fear. His tense muscles ached, his body curled painfully into a fetal position.

3

He wanted to scream, make them stop this one-way hell ride. But he knew they wouldn't, that it was too late now. He'd gone too far, knew too much.

Harding Scott swallowed the bile in his throat and yielded to his fate.

CHAPTER ONE

He'd done it, all right. Killed him in cold blood. End of story. Or so it should have been.

Metro Toronto Police Detective Stevie Houston wearily rubbed her forehead. Her hand came away sweaty.

Four hours of late-night interrogation had sapped her like a sponge. Her thoughts turned bitter as she looked across the scratched table at the smelly, grubby form slumped in the chair. She didn't need this bullshit. Her partner, Ted Jovanowski, a long-time homicide veteran, leaned against the wall behind her, arms lazily hugging his broad chest, his jowly face set like day-old plaster of Paris.

Stevie testily drummed her fingers on the faded tabletop. *Jesus, now he's talking about his sorry childhood!*

She couldn't see his mouth, which was hidden beneath a filthy, wiry beard, but it had to be moving at a furious pace to keep up with the flood of words pouring from him. He'd felt compelled to tell them every detail of his murderous impulse, right down to what he'd eaten that day, where his garbage-hunting travels had taken him, whom he'd talked to and what he'd said, and now his whole bloody life story. They wanted a statement and were getting a nonstop autobiography.

Earlier in the evening, Mr. Verbose had stabbed another homeless man in the throat, killing him almost instantly. Nothing glorious about it, no movie-of-the-week in the making. The two had been fighting over a half bottle of whiskey. There was a reliable witness, a bloody knife, and the confession of the century. It wasn't unusual for a murderer to confess so handily. Sometimes it was guilt, sometimes just a pair of seemingly sympathetic ears, or sometimes the knowledge that a confession would more quickly lead to a meal and a bed. And in this case, there was no sparkling future to protect, no promise of a better life ahead.

Now Stevie and Jovanowski were compelled to let him say his piece. Though it gave the detectives an open-and-shut case, there was about as much challenge to it as writing a parking ticket.

Stevie focused on the smoke-yellowed ceiling tiles, tuning out the monologue and letting the video

6

camera record the wondrous event. Finally, she could take it no more, her volatile temper throbbing in her temples and threatening to erupt. Abruptly she stalked from the room, slamming the door behind her.

Christ. She needed a drink. She was tired of being handed every shitty case that came down the pipe, even though she was still considered a homicide rookie. She was better than this. She knew it, her coworkers knew it, and her inspector, Jack McLemore, knew it too. But there was no sign of her punishment letting up anytime soon. Nine months ago, just a month into her homicide career, she'd screwed up big-time. Oh, she'd solved the case, and practically by herself, but had nearly got a civilian killed in the process. And not just any civilian, but the love of her life, Dr. Jade Agawa-Garneau.

Jovanowski was still paying the price too. Just hours after he'd checked himself out of the hospital and still on sick leave from a heart attack, he'd showed up in the nick of time to save Stevie's ass and Jade's too. The whole unorthodox event was about as popular with her department as an overnight doughnut shop with a broken coffeemaker.

A slack smile spread across Jovanowski's face as he joined Stevie, his reddened eyes betraying his exhaustion. "I'd say we've both had enough. We can finish this in the morning, and in the meantime, let's pray the asshole gets laryngitis."

Stevie sighed, sorry for her impatience and regretting for the millionth time that it was her fault they were both on their inspector's shit list. She tried not to notice the resigned look in Jovanowski's eyes every day, the slumping of his shoulders, the perpetual drag in his step.

He used to be such a fighter and would have easily told McLemore to shove these kindergarten cases up his ass. But not anymore, not since the heart attack and Stevie's failed heroics. Someday, he'd be his old self again, she kept telling herself. They just needed a good case.

"C'mon kid, go on home to Jade."

Stevie smiled. Her heart cartwheeled every time her partner mentioned her lover, for it was another sign of his acceptance of them. They'd told him just before Christmas. He struggled silently with it for a couple of weeks, then sheepishly showed up at their door Christmas day, gifts in hand and a big, silly grin on his wide face. They were his family now, his wife having divorced him years ago. He kept Stevie's little secret at work and, like a big brother, fought fiercely for her honor any time a coworker tried to defame her.

Someday, maybe she'd come out at work, but not yet. She was already in the doghouse; she didn't want to be out the bloody door and busted down to traffic division!

"You're right, Ted. I'll see you tomorrow."

It was 2:00 A.M. by the time Stevie tiptoed upstairs and into the bedroom of the four-story, Victorian duplex they shared on Sackville Street, just north of Carleton in Toronto's Cabbagetown. The neighborhood was suitably upscale, suitably yuppie, and more than sufficiently gay.

A bedside lamp clicked on as she softly shut the door.

"I'm sorry, honey, I didn't mean to wake you," Stevie whispered, then foolishly wondered why she was whispering since Jade was already awake.

Jade smiled, her shoulder-length, black hair tousled sleepily around her. She'd been steadily having her once waist-length hair cut shorter during their nine months together, but hadn't yet taken Stevie up on her dare to cut it really short.

Stevie kissed Jade briefly on the lips, knowing the toothpaste wasn't doing a very good job of masking the bourbon on her breath. She sat down on the bed. God, Jade was beautiful. Stevie breathed deeply. Though grumpy, tired, and limp from liquor, Stevie felt the familiar stirring of lust. She reached for Jade's smooth, eternally-tanned cheek, wanting to curl right up inside those big green eyes sleepily questioning her. She still marveled at how lucky she'd been to snag such a catch, sometimes still couldn't figure out what Jade saw in her.

"You're home late."

Stevie nodded wearily. "Long night."

"Anything exciting?" Jade asked hopefully.

Stevie barely shook her head, then began tugging at her pants and socks. The sound of the cold February wind rattling the window sent a spontaneous shiver through her. "Same old shit. Some dirtbag who thinks his life story is next year's Oscar winner."

Jade touched Stevie's well-muscled forearm and began stroking it with an implied an invitation.

Deciphering the unspoken language, Stevie smiled, regret heavy in her voice. "It's 2:00 A.M., luv. Don't you have to be up in a few hours?"

Jade nodded. "Sorry. It's just that, you know, it's been a week."

Stevie smiled ruefully. "I know. But the weekend's almost here and we're both off. Is it a date?"

Jade grinned enthusiastically, her eyes already making love to Stevie's body. Sex had steadily slipped on the list of priorities the last few weeks, their work schedules demanding more energy than they had a right to. But that was married life.

"What are you doing up anyway?" Stevie scrunched her shirt into a ball and lazily tossed it to the floor.

Jade's eyes admired the flinching muscles. She liked the fact that Stevie was five inches taller — about five-foot-nine — stocky and well toned. And it was still a thrill whenever Stevie picked her up and tossed her on the bed or couch in a fit of play. Oh well, she sighed quietly. Tomorrow night she'd feast.

"I dozed for a while, but I've been thinking about this autopsy case I'm reviewing."

"Why, is it a tricky one?"

Jade shrugged T-shirted shoulders as Stevie climbed over her and scrambled between the flannel sheets. "Not tricky really, but fascinating. It's from four years ago."

"Four years ago? What'd you do, dig up an old body?"

Jade wrinkled her nose, a look of repulsion contorting her face. "No, thank god. Just reviewing the files at the request of a private citizen. It's my first case as a private consult, actually."

Jade, a forensic pathologist with the Ontario Coroner's Office, was excited by the news that staff pathologists could now be hired to review private cases, as long as it was on their own time.

Stevie yawned, not meaning to look bored. "That's great, hon. It's interesting, you say?"

Jade clicked the bedside lamp off. Reaching under the covers, she intertwined her fingers with Stevie's. "A police detective was found dead in her car in a remote spot. It was ruled a suicide, but it's not adding up."

Stevie's voice grew faint. "I don't remember any Toronto dicks turning up dead four years ago."

"No, she was from Shelton. You know, that little city a couple of hours east of here on the Canada-U.S. border."

The hand in Jade's had gone limp. Stevie was snoring softly.

Stevie reread her report on last night's confession, double-checking for errors, her eyes discriminately roving across the computer screen. She didn't need the department's brass or the provincial prosecutor chewing her ass for making mistakes on such a Mickey Mouse case. She laced her fingers behind her head, sighed grumpily. She was quickly losing the concentration battle.

Stevie closed her eyes, and, as usual when her mind slowed its frenetic pace, Jade floated into her thoughts. Her quick smile curled into a frown as she remembered how she'd rudely fallen asleep in the middle of conversation. *Shit.* Maybe she could grab some flowers on the way home or a bottle of Jade's favorite wine. She'd need to kiss up.

What was it Jade had been talking about? Something about reviewing a case out of Shelton, a dead detective.

Shelton struck a nagging chord in Stevie; she was

sure she'd heard the city mentioned around the office nearly a year ago, around the time she'd started in homicide. Her curiosity being the diversion she needed, Stevie aborted out of her report. With new vigor, she tapped into the search-and-find program, typing the word *Shelton* at the keyword prompt.

She waited while the program searched all the Metro Toronto Police files, then opened the one file it found.

So that was where she'd heard the name. Two of her fellow homicide detectives, Murphy and White, were the primaries on the case of a Shelton detective found dumped in a trash bin in Toronto, a bullet in his head. But it was from just over a year ago — last January — not four years ago.

And it was a he — Harding Scott — not a female cop as Jade had said.

Stevie leaned in closer to the monitor, her insatiable curiosity piqued. A witness had described what looked like a carjacking early one morning, with two burly men throwing Scott into the trunk. One man took off in another car, the other left the scene in Scott's car. But it was dark, and the witness only saw the tail end of things from her apartment window across the street. Descriptions of the characters were pretty much nonexistent, and Scott's car had been found abandoned and trashed a few days later, Stevie read. A few latent prints had been found inside, but they hadn't matched with any known criminal in the national police computer system.

The case was still unsolved and tagged as active, though Stevie knew that was crap. She read how there had been six detectives on the case at first with only

White and Murphy remaining, but it was probably about fifth on their priority list by now.

Stevie stood, squinted across the large, third-floor homicide squad room. No sign of Murphy and White. She made a mental note to find out more. And as for her little honey . . . Stevie grinned. This time she wouldn't fall asleep in the middle of her story.

CHAPTER TWO

Stevie cleared the plates from the table and haphazardly stacked them on the kitchen counter. She was no housekeeper, for sure. Not much of a cook either. She frowned, glanced at her hands. Oh well, she was good for at least *one* thing. She grinned mischievously.

She joined Jade in the living room, dialing the volume down on Jade's Motown music as she glided by.

"Now can we talk about it, please?" Stevie's

question was one of pretend deference. "Have I suitably romanced you enough?"

Jade crooked a scornful eyebrow, hesitated as if grading Stevie's actions. "For now," she smiled slyly. "But there better be more romance left in you than a candlelight dinner and wine."

Stevie laughed and tilted her wineglass in a silent salute.

"OK, my sweet, shoot."

Stevie had earlier promised Jade not to quiz her on her private case until after dinner. And not for the whole evening, Jade had sternly warned her. They had plans, plans that didn't include much talking.

"So tell me all about it, every detail."

Jade took a deep breath, knowing Stevie indeed meant every last detail. When her lover got into that cop mode, her inquisitive mind would soak up every fiber of information, decipher every nuance, and file away each unanswered question for later reference. Jade smiled inwardly and felt a surge of pride at the sight of Stevie's brown eyes turned dark and serious, strong square jaw jutting out, body stiff and leaning slightly forward in anticipation. Stevie was a good cop, but if she didn't adapt to playing by the rules, Jade feared hers would be a short career.

Jade reached for a thick file folder on the glass coffee table in front of them. "Gina Lynne Walters, thirty-nine years old. Detective with the Shelton Police force."

Stevie's nose wrinkled skeptically. "How long was she a detective?"

Jade bit back a smile at Stevie's transparent competitiveness. It was a cop thing, Jade had learned.

Cops liked to compare biceps, war stories, commendations, anything to prove to one another they were the toughest, the best.

"Let's see. It says here she started in uniform at twenty-six, moved to detective branch just a year before she died."

Stevie nodded sternly, obviously satisfied this dead woman didn't have anything on her. Not many would, since Stevie had made homicide just under a year ago at the age of thirty.

Jade scanned the sheets of paper, firing off the information. "Found dead in her car in a field just outside of Shelton, December 23, just over four years ago. Ruled a suicide. Service revolver, a .38 Smith & Wesson, found on the floor by her feet. It was missing one round, gunshot wounds in the head — one entry, one exit. Typical messy scene."

"And you're thinking it wasn't suicide?"

Jade leaned back, her body relaxing but her eyes hard. "I have lots of problems with this thing. First of all, the entrance wound is in the forehead, over the left eye, in the frontal lobe." Jade pointed to a spot about two inches above the outer corner of her left eye. "Hell of a place to put a gun to your own head when you're right-handed."

Stevie's eyes narrowed, her mouth tightening with visible distaste.

"Wait, it gets better. The bullet was fired almost straight down into her skull at about a 45-degree angle, the bullet traversing left to right and exiting on the opposite side of her head, at the base of her skull."

Jade pulled the crime scene photos from the folder.

"Gray matter from the cerebellum was found on the back of her seat."

Stevie raised an invisible gun to her head, crossing her right hand over her face in imitation of the angle. "Jesus, that's uncomfortable. What about the gun ending up on the floor?"

Jade shrugged. "Could happen. Once she'd fired it, the impact of the gun firing and the jolting of her body could have sent the thing flying. But the really interesting thing is that her prints weren't found on the gun. It's as though the thing was wiped clean."

"It should have had some kind of prints, even partial ones or smudges." Stevie's voice rose an octave like an excited child's. She loved hashing out cases with Jade, their minds feeding off each other. It was almost as good as sex. "It was her gun, for crissakes. At the start and finish of every shift she would be handling that gun."

"Exactly. And there's more. No powder residue was found on her hands."

Stevie nodded impatiently. She was not surprised, since Walters's prints hadn't been found on the gun either. Not only was it extremely unlikely no prints would be on the gun, but residue from the gun's escaping gases should have been left on her hand — if she'd fired it.

Jade tossed a couple of close-up photos onto Stevie's lap, knowing what she was about to say would send Stevie through the roof. "See that entry hole? There's no tattooing or burn marks from the muzzle. Without those marks, there's no way a gun was fired at extreme close range."

"Then Walters would have needed a four-foot-long

arm to shoot herself on the opposite side of her head from that distance away." Stevie shook her head in disbelief. "Christ, I can't believe this. How could they have missed all this and called it a suicide?"

Stevie hated sloppy police work as much as Jade hated botched forensic work.

Jade shook her head in disgust. "The pathologist wasn't trained in forensics. For all I know this was his one and only gunshot death. He was a family doctor and just did the occasional autopsy. He retired six months later and died of a heart attack last year. I checked."

"What else do you know about the gun?"

"No question it'd been fired. Gunshot residue was found on the muzzle. But what's interesting is that there was no blowback reportedly found on the muzzle."

Jade didn't need to explain to Stevie that a gun, when fired at very close range, sucks up things like blood, hair, or tissue into its barrel. No traces of blowback was just more confirmation that the gun had been fired at a range too far away for Walters to have shot herself.

"The bullet was too fragmented to tell if it'd been fired by her gun," Jade continued, "but it appeared to be the same caliber."

Stevie's eyes danced over an invisible horizon. "So someone used her own gun on her as she sat in the car."

"Or they used a similar gun on her, then took hers, fired off a round somewhere in that field, then threw it back inside the car," Jade interjected. "All without leaving any prints, of course."

Jade began assembling the photos and papers to

stuff back in the file. "There's one more thing. When the car was found, the driver's window was almost completely down."

Stevie stood, her pacing meant to vent her energy. "Like she was talking to someone. Why else would you sit there with the window down in December?"

"Exactly. But all of it seemed to elude the authorities. There was no inquiry, no nothing. Just a simple case of a burned-out cop who turned to suicide."

"Yeah, right," Stevie spat. "What the hell was wrong with the cops investigating this thing? I mean, she was one of theirs, for crissakes."

Jade shrugged and reached for Stevie's hand as she marched by, enveloped in her own thoughts.

Stevie was burning up inside at the thought that one of the brotherhood had died suspiciously, and yet the Shelton cops didn't seem to give a shit. At least somebody did, though. "Does she have family? Is that who you're consulting for?"

Jade's look was one of mock scolding. "You know I can't tell you that." She looked quickly around for invisible spies and brought her hand up to her mouth to whisper. "The woman she lived with hired me."

Stevie grinned. "Lover?"

"Don't know, never met her, but could be."

"So why now, after four years?"

"Good question, Stevie. And she's a little nervous, almost like she's scared. Wants to keep it all between her and me, so don't go blabbing."

Stevie sat down again, pensively sipping from her wine glass. "Last January, did you autopsy a guy named Harding Scott?"

Jade laughed. "C'mon hon, you know I don't

remember names. Bullet holes, knife wounds, bashed heads — those I remember."

Stevie rolled her eyes. "How silly of me. Okay, bullet hole to the back of the head, found in a Toronto Dumpster after a supposed carjacking. And, he was a detective. Guess from where?"

"Oh no, not from Shelton. God, this sounds like a bad movie, doesn't it? No, I didn't work on that one, but I remember hearing about it now. I never knew he was from Shelton, though."

"Don't you think it's funny that two detectives from a small-city police force turn up dead within three years of each other? And both are unsolved?"

"Hey, it's got me busting a gut."

Stevie frowned good-naturedly. "You know what I mean."

"Yes, you're right, it is pretty weird."

Stevie jumped up and made a beeline for the phone.

"What are you doing?" Jade demanded, agitation in her voice.

"Calling Ted. Maybe we can do something with this."

"Whoa there, Tex." Jade knew her little nickname would stop Stevie in her tracks. Stevie had hated that name when Jade first began calling her it. Of course, that was almost a year ago, when they didn't like each other. Now Stevie tolerated it. "I told you not to be blabbing about this case. And besides, I've got plans for you tonight."

Stevie made a show of setting the receiver down slowly. "All right, all right. If I must," she winked teasingly. "But I'm going to phone him later and ask him over for breakfast tomorrow."

"C'mere," Jade winked coquettishly. Her hand slid down the front of her shirt, tauntingly relieving another button of its task.

Stevie grinned and swaggered back to Jade in her best John Wayne imitation. "Teasing me, huh? You know what I do to little ladies who tease me?"

"Why, don't tell me, show me, my little stud woman," Jade giggled breathlessly in her best Southern accent.

"All right, but you asked for it." With that Stevie leaped on top of Jade and began tickling her relentlessly.

Jade giggled and fought for breath, trying but failing to push the heavier Stevie off her. "I'll get you," she managed between gasps. "I'll get you while you're sleeping, I swear!"

"Promises, promises." Stevie suddenly stopped her impish attack and caressed Jade's forehead, sweeping the soft hair away. She couldn't imagine anyone more perfect looking. Jade's cultural background — French and Ojibwa Indian — made for a breathtaking combination of slightly tanned skin, round green eyes, prominent cheekbones, long straight nose, and a strong jaw. She turned heads when she entered a room, and it left Stevie both proud and damned scared at the same time.

"Whatcha thinking about?" Jade smiled up at her.

"About how much I love you." Stevie kissed her then, the softness of their lips and the smoothness of their faces melting like butter.

Stevie's tongue traced a sugary path down Jade's long, exposed neck, stopping at the hollow of flesh above her collarbone, where her lips sucked playfully.

No more talk of murder and bullet holes tonight. Jade had called this one right. No more talk about anything, Stevie thought devilishly as she devoured this dessert called Jade.

CHAPTER THREE

It couldn't be Stevie's imagination. There was a glint in Jovanowksi's eyes. Not exactly a raging fire, but definitely a spark.

"So what do you think, Ted?"

The burly detective swallowed a mouthful of scrambled egg and nodded to Stevie. "I'd say Shelton sounds like an interesting place to visit. Maybe have a little chat with the next-of-kin of Harding Scott and Gina Walters."

"Wait a minute, you two," Jade cut in, her hand raised to forestall the protests she knew would come.

"I really don't think this roommate of Walters would be all that thrilled to sit down with you two. If she'd wanted to proceed further with this, she would have. As it is, she won't be pleased when she finds out I've passed all of this on to the police."

"I'll take responsibility for that," Stevie shrugged. "And anyway, isn't it your duty or something to report this?"

Jade frowned. She knew Stevie well enough to know that if you threw her the ball, she'd not only run off with it, but go for the slam dunk. But dammit, it was her court and her ball, and Stevie would just have to remember that.

"No, it's not my duty. That autopsy followed the Coroner's Act to the letter, and the police have already investigated. I'm acting as a private consult, and I just happen to disagree with the original conclusions. It's up to Dana Jeffries to pursue it further, since she hired me."

Stevie sidled up to Jade and planted a flamboyant kiss on her cheek. "C'mon, honey," she implored sweetly. "Help us out here. We have to talk to Jeffries as part of our investigation of the Scott murder. And if you can warm her up for us, she'll be more cooperative."

Jovanowski concentrated on the idle ceiling fan, his face blushing at the little show of affection before him.

Jade smiled reluctantly, her head slowly shaking in resignation. Would she ever learn to say no to Stevie? Probably not. "She's coming to see me next Tuesday to get my report. I'll tell her how wonderful you are, and then maybe we can meet you for coffee."

"Yes!" Stevie grinned and pumped the air with her fist. "I knew you'd help." She grabbed Jade and dipped her in her best Fred Astaire imitation, both of them caught up in Stevie's enthusiasm.

Jovanowski, his face brick red, coughed in embarrassment. "Before you get too carried away, Tex, we're not exactly officially on this Scott case. There's the little matter of Murphy and White. They're not gonna like us stepping all over their case, even though they haven't done diddly with it."

Stevie nodded soberly, her playfulness gone. "We'll have to be careful with them. But we would be doing them a favor since it's unsolved. And since we've been feeding at the bottom of the tank lately anyway, it's only fitting." Stevie's smile hardened into a scowl. "What about Inspector McLemore? He'll never go for it."

Jovanowski winked conspiratorially. "It's about time I raised holy hell with him about something."

Jade, still playing the stern one, glared at Jovanowski. "You just be careful. You're still recovering from your heart attack, so don't go getting yourself all worked up." Jade felt like a mother reining in her straying children, and she worried about Jovanowski's health. He'd lost some weight and quit smoking in recent months, and while it felt good to see the two of them excited about work for a change, she worried about the stress that a challenging case would place on Jovanowski, who, in his early fifties, was no spring chicken. He was eligible to retire in three years, and Jade hoped his career wouldn't completely suck up the best years of his life.

The veteran detective saluted. "Yes, doctor. In fact, I'll subject my body to your capable hands any time."

They laughed nervously. Stevie and Jade knew Jovanowski had always found Jade attractive — like who didn't — and there were still times he seemed a little shell-shocked that she would choose to love a woman over a man.

Stevie — handsomely masculine, moody, aggressive — Jovanowski could understand. But Jade. She was so beautiful, desirable, had even been married for a while. How could she be that way? he wondered time and again, and his face didn't hide his perplexity very well. It came out in the stolen looks — the way he would appraise her as if appraising some exotic, abstract piece of art, afraid to get too close to it, but wanting to understand it.

The two women studied Jovanowski as he stared into his coffee cup, the furrows in his forehead deeply etched. He shifted in his seat and noisily cleared his throat, his eyes still riveted on his cup. "So, like, you two just don't like men, or what?" he asked quietly.

Stevie and Jade exchanged amused glances. He'd always been afraid to ask questions, or even bring the subject up, since they'd told him their news in mid-December.

Jade, more at ease with words and emotions than Stevie, took the seat beside Jovanowski and clasped her hand over his. "It's not that we don't like men, Ted. Have we ever made you feel that we dislike you? Because if we have, we —"

"No, you haven't." His eyes hesitated, slowly lifted to hers. "It's just, why would you pick, you know, women? Like, what's wrong with men?"

Jade laughed. "Oh, Ted, there's nothing at all wrong with men. It's exactly the same as why you find women attractive, and choose women to have relationships with. And it's not as though you hate men, right? You just don't want to sleep with them."

Jovanowski's checks began to flush all over again, but his eyes were firm. A slow smile began to flow across his arid features.

Stevie winked and slapped her coworker on the back. "Hey, Ted. Anytime you want to go girl watching, you just say the word."

Jade stood, hands firmly planted on her narrow hips in mock reproachment. "Watch all you want, my little cowgirl. But just remember, you're married."

Stevie cursed quietly as she climbed out of the unmarked Chevy Caprice and stepped squarely in a slush-filled pothole. She yanked at the collar of her leather outback coat, trying to shield herself from Lake Ontario's biting wind as she walked south on Church Street. She felt her hair, so straight and fine, being lifted by the wind as if she'd stuck her finger in an electrical socket.

Jade had phoned Stevie minutes earlier to give her the OK to meet with her and Dana Jeffries. They had decided in advance to leave Jovanowski behind, for if Jeffries had indeed been the lesbian lover of Gina Walters, Stevie and Jade had a much better chance of getting her to open up without the presence of the dour-looking veteran detective.

Stevie caught Jade's eye as she hung her coat up

inside the entrance of the Village Bistro. She hastily raked her fingers through her hopelessly ruffled hair on the way to their table.

"Hi, I'm Detective Stephanie Houston," Stevie smiled, extending her hand to the strawberry blond, slightly plump stranger seated next to Jade. "It's nice to meet you."

Stevie was surprised at the firmness of Dana Jeffries's handshake, half expecting someone skittish and reticent by the way Jade had earlier described her. She was also younger than Stevie had envisioned, probably mid-thirties. And though her smile wasn't much of an effort, Jeffries's cobalt-blue eyes were resolute and sincere as she returned the introduction.

Stevie buttoned her black sports jacket as she sat opposite Jeffries, making sure her shoulder holster and .40-caliber pistol were hidden. She hated having to wear her gun on occasions like this, times when she wanted to come across more as a friend than a cop, though she had to concede there were plenty of times when signs of authority had their advantages. Nevertheless, on duty she was compelled to wear the side arm.

It was well past lunch, but Stevie ordered a garden salad for herself and coffees all around.

"I'm sorry we have to meet under these circumstances." Stevie smiled again, sweeping a stray lock of short, brown hair from her forehead. "Jade's explained why I'm here?"

Jeffries nodded grimly. "She's told me she thinks Gina was . . . murdered." Her voice wavered, but, with effort, she swallowed visibly and squared her shoulders. "Dr. Agawa-Garneau's talked some sense

28

into me . . . you know, about proceeding with this thing. See, I've always known it wasn't suicide."

"How have you known?" Stevie asked forcefully, wanting to see what this woman was made of.

The determined glare and the twitching of Dana Jeffries's jaw muscles reassured Stevie that this woman was no cream puff. They could count on her.

"Gina would never do that to me. She loved being a cop; she was happy with her life. It was almost Christmas, for godsakes. She would have said goodbye." Her eyes began to moisten, her voice cracking. Stevie and Jade exchanged knowing glances. Just roommates? *Not!*

"The Shelton police report said she was having trouble adjusting to her new role as a detective," Stevie continued. "She'd been continually asking the brass to put her back in uniform."

They were silent as the waitress set down their steaming mugs and Stevie's salad.

"That's true," Jeffries confirmed. "She felt her coworkers were continually stonewalling her in her investigations, trying to make it rough for her. She could have continued handling it, but she figured she didn't need that crap in her life, you know?"

Stevie certainly knew something about that. In her first couple of months in homicide, she'd had plenty of second thoughts. It wasn't easy for any woman in policing.

"The report also said she was having some sort of personality adjustments in her private life," Stevie said, her subdued tone respectful despite this intrusion into their personal lives. "What was that supposed to mean?"

Dana Jeffries absently stirred her coffee, her eyes averted and unfocused. When she finally looked first to Jade, then to Stevie, it was to gauge their trustworthiness. Her fingers tightly clutched the spoon, her knuckles whitening. "Gina and I were lovers. We'd been together five years. Her department knew it. They didn't like it. Shelton's a small city. People talked, especially her coworkers. They harassed her constantly about it."

"Enough to make her want to kill herself?" Jade gently inquired.

Jeffries firmly shook her head. "Never. She was stronger than that."

Jade watched Stevie play with her salad and took it as her cue to continue. "Did she despair about her lesbianism? Because even though she loved you, there may have been a part of her that just couldn't accept what she was."

The woman's eyes began to fill again, her lips trembling in silent protest. "She did love me, and she was comfortable with who she was. She did not kill herself because she was gay."

Stevie believed her. "Do you have any idea who might have killed her or why?"

Dana Jeffries's face was tortured, her eyes blankly fixed on a distant wall. "You don't know how many nights I've stayed awake the past four years trying to figure that out. I know she was working on some big case before she died."

Stevie's eyebrows shot up in alarm. "What case?"

Jeffries shook her head in exasperation. "I don't know; she wouldn't tell me. Just said it was really big, that it would either wreck her career forever or make her a hero. I know she stayed awake a lot of nights worrying about it."

Stevie's gut told her it must have been one hell of a big case indeed. Yet the police reports made no mention of that angle being investigated as a possible cause of her death, even if they did believe it was suicide.

As if reading her mind, Jeffries said, "I even went to the chief with my concerns about it after she died."

"And?"

Jeffries's shrug was that of a beaten woman. "He said her cases had been passed on and that they were no cause for alarm."

"And did you believe him?" Jade asked.

"No."

Stevie set her fork down, swallowing her burgeoning frustration. She couldn't imagine just giving up so easily if Jade had been murdered. Hell, an army wouldn't be able to stop her from traveling to the ends of the earth until she found whoever was responsible and tore them apart with her bare hands.

Like a fierce kick in the chest, a flashback of that terrible night last spring on the beach hit Stevie, sucking the breath from her lungs. Fuzzily, she could see Jade, crumpled, a knife about to be plunged into her, and herself standing there, too far away, knowing that anything she could do would be too late.

She stuffed her trembling hands into her lap. God, how close she'd come then to losing Jade, to losing all meaning in her life. Unfortunately, she could all too well imagine what Dana Jeffries was going through.

"Why are you suddenly doing something about it now?" Stevie's voice simmered.

Jeffries sipped her coffee slowly, her broad shoulders stiff against the unspoken criticism. "I hired Jade because I want some facts, something I can look at at night that says 'yes, Dana, you were right.' I almost went crazy at the thought that nothing was being done, that Gina would forever be known in town as that wacko cop who killed herself. But Harding promised me he wouldn't give up, and now I can't either. Neither of them would want that."

Stevie's mouth fell open in ill-concealed surprise. "Harding Scott?"

Jeffries nodded. "He was actually the only person on the whole force Gina liked. But when he was killed last year, I got afraid."

"And now?" Jade asked.

A slight shrug. "Now it's time for me to get on with my life, to close this chapter. I've decided to move here to Toronto soon. Shelton can go to hell for all I care."

CHAPTER FOUR

The suspense was killing Stevie, as it was meant to. Her foot began impatiently tapping like a metronome.

Inspector Jack McLemore, his dark eyes glacial, hadn't moved a muscle in his imposed silence. He seemed not to breathe, looking like an Eaton Centre mannequin in his custom-cut suit and plastic hair.

How does he keep every hair in place? Stevie wondered in sarcastic amusement for the umpteenth time. If her childhood Ken doll had aged, it'd surely look just like Jack McLemore — if she'd had a Ken doll, that is. Stevie had been more of a G.I. Joe girl.

Jovanowski, sitting stiffly beside her, stared somewhere past their inspector in bored detachment, long used to his scolding games. They had asked, practically begged, to take over the Harding Scott case. Their inspector was letting them sweat it out, and both had every intention of taking this symbolic spanking stoically.

"How can I be sure you two aren't going to fuck up?"

Stevie always found it absurd when her inspector swore, for it was so uncharacteristic of his banker looks and educated clip. It wasn't uncommon anymore for young officers like Stevie to have a university degree, but McLemore's growing collection of degrees and certificates meant this was a man on the move. He was not to be taken lightly. Since joining homicide, Stevie had certainly put his patience to the test, stretching it like a rubber band. She glanced sideways at her partner.

"Inspector, I can assure you that Stevie and I have no intention of doing anything but solving this case." Jovanowski's voice was dry and taut, as though it might crack with a little more force. It was obvious he hated this kowtowing bullshit.

McLemore waited again, steepled his cigarette-yellowed fingers — his one physical detraction — and glared, unblinking. "I'll tell you something. You're lucky Murphy and White are anxious to drop this thing. They're only too happy to serve you two up to the media's scrutiny over why we can't catch a cop killer. They're rather amused by your request."

Stevie's grip on the arm of her chair relaxed. So

he was going to give them one more chance. The portentous drumming of his fingers on the desktop and the clenched jaw told her that if they failed, it would be early retirement for Jovanowski and patrol for Stevie. No third chances, no better luck next time. This was it.

They rose in unison, McLemore following them to the door. "I want to be informed of every move in advance, and everything gets first approval by me."

"Yes, sir," Stevie nodded, swallowing the mixed emotions lumping in her throat. She desperately wanted back in the game, but was she ready for sudden-death overtime? Now she wasn't so sure. She'd grown sedentary sitting on the bench.

After they'd gone, McLemore perched on the edge of his desk, long fingers stroking his smooth chin. He had to do something with this dead-end case. And if Houston and Jovanowski somehow pulled this off with their unorthodox techniques, he'd look brilliant. On the other hand, if they didn't, he'd look like the biggest jerk on the whole force.

Stevie struggled to get out of bed, her legs leaden, the weight of an invisible boulder crushing her chest. She sank back into the pillow, its plushness failing to soften the thunder and lightning storm going on in her head.

"Fuck," she cursed weakly. The bedside clock was a blur. She should be at work. She didn't even remember Jade leaving for work. *Christ.* It felt like the worst hangover in the world, yet she hadn't had a drop of booze.

Her second attempt to get out of bed was just as doomed. She floated on a foggy sea of nothingness, felt the mist of fever on her face — delirium and nausea a wave away. It was sometime later when the ring of the phone roused her. Her sweat-slicked hand reached for the bedside receiver.

"Yeah," she mumbled weakly, her tongue thick and swollen.

"Stevie, is that you?" barked Jovanowski. "What the hell are you doing?"

Stevie forced her eyes open. *Goddamn.* It felt like someone had glued them shut. "I . . . I dunno. Sleeping."

"What the hell's wrong with you? Are you sick?"

Stevie's mind felt like porridge as she strained for an answer. She didn't hear the click of the phone line, left the receiver dangling as she fell back into the murky pool.

She woke to a cool cloth on her head. Gentle, competent hands prodded her.

"Stevie, honey, it's me. Just lie still."

A thermometer rested under Stevie's tongue and Jade stroked her fiery cheek. Stevie strained to smile at Jade's warming presence.

Jade's forehead crinkled with concern as she plucked the thermometer out. "You've got a fever of a hundred and two, hon. You're very sick. Now open up again, just for a sec."

A small light illuminated Stevie's reddened throat,

Jade reading it like a landmark on a familiar highway. "Your throat's infected. You've probably got strep. I'm going out to get you some antibiotics."

Stevie was too sick to make a joke about Jade having the chance to work on a live patient for once, and protested instead. "But, work. I —"

"Shh. Don't try to talk. I'll be right back, and I'll make you the best damn chicken soup you've ever had."

Stevie could hear the muffled voices of Jade and Jovanowski outside her closed door. Their voices were harsh and hurried, argumentative. Finally, Jade entered the bedroom, shutting the door behind her.

Stevie pushed herself up to a sitting position. "What's going on?" *Jesus.* It hurt just to talk.

"Ted and I were just having a discussion about you."

Stevie's eyebrows dipped skeptically as Jade sat down on the edge of the bed. It sure as hell didn't sound like just a discussion.

"We both agreed you're not going with him to Shelton tomorrow."

Stevie's face darkened, the promise of a temper tantrum looming. They'd been planning this day trip for days. They were going to talk to Harding Scott's son and the brass at the Shelton police department. "Like hell I'm not."

Jade's stubbornness matched Stevie's. "You're far too sick. You're taking a couple of days off, and that's all there is to it. Doctor's orders. You push it now and you'll end up with pneumonia or bronchial asthma. This bloody case can wait for you."

Stevie felt powerless against the steam building inside, the pulse of air bubbling to the surface, the inevitable eruption. Keeping her temper under control wasn't one of her stronger points. "You'd like me off the whole goddamned case, wouldn't you? In fact, you'd like me to get out of policing altogether. Why don't you just admit it?"

Jade's eyes instantly turned a stormy sea-green. Stevie had pushed that one button — her policing career — that was a sure guarantee to send them both over the precipice. "I'm not getting into this with you now, Stevie. You're tired, you're sick, and you're on medication. Now get some sleep."

Jade made a hasty departure, wondering gloomily if Stevie's career would forever be a bone of contention between them. She wanted Stevie to be happy and she was proud of her, but she was also afraid for her. Afraid she was one of those people who needed that constant element of danger in their life, always living on the edge, redefining the limits.

Not one to let a little infection keep her down, Stevie compromised with Jade. While Jovanowski spent the day in Shelton, Stevie worked the phone from her bedroom and read every scrap of paper in the Harding Scott case file.

He'd died quickly, a 9 mm pistol shot once at close range into the back of his head, execution style. No idea where the actual shooting had taken place since his body was found in a Toronto Dumpster. The car, trashed and with its stereo missing, was found in an empty parking lot on the edge of the city. For a while at least, Scott had been in that trunk while he was still alive. There was no blood, but plenty of fibers from the clothes he was still wearing when his rotting corpse was found.

Stevie closed her eyes, trying to imagine the fear that must have gripped Scott as he lay scrunched inside that trunk, well aware that death was his destination. He had to have known this was no random carjacking just as she knew it now. This was no amateur job. He'd been executed. The car stereo was missing, probably in an attempt to throw investigators off. But Stevie wasn't buying it. It was far too violent a method for ripping off a crappy stereo.

What bothered Stevie were the latent prints they'd been unable to match to any of the thousands of criminals on file. Why weren't any of Scott's fingerprints found inside the car? And why just four prints on the steering wheel? There were none on the gearshift, none on the door handles. The car was clean but for those four prints. Wiped clean, just like Gina Walters's gun had been wiped clean.

Fever and questions burned in Stevie's mind. Why would two detectives from a small force end up murdered? There must have been something they'd been working on, some explosive case. Yet the Shelton reports indicated they'd been investigating little more than forged checks, stolen bicycles, kiddie diddling — run-of-the-mill stuff. And Dana Jeffries really had no idea what her lover had been up to.

Maybe the two murders weren't connected at all, Stevie mused, playing her own devil's advocate. Someone obviously wanted Gina dead. But why was Scott not killed until three years later? And why was he suddenly deemed a threat anyway? Here was a guy who'd had a heart attack about eighteen months before he died. He was then off work for a year, and was still on light duties at the time of his death.

Stevie picked up the phone and dialed Dana Jeffries's number, catching her on the second ring.

Stevie had to work at convincing Dana it was really her, her voice croaking.

"You said Gina had been working on an important case before she died. Did she have any files, notebooks, anything work-related at home?"

A slow expulsion of breath. "She had a filing cabinet in the garage that she kept some work stuff in. But after she died, I gave it to the police department, since it was police business . . . I guess that was a mistake, maybe."

"Look, don't do this to yourself, Dana. You just did what you thought was right. Was there anything else, any other personal papers you kept that might give us some clue as to what Gina was working on?"

Dana was quiet as she thought. "No, I don't think . . . oh yeah, wait. Her personal journal." Dana's voice had picked up, seemingly glad to finally be of help. "I lent it to Harding Scott when he was recovering from his heart attack — he asked to look at it and gave it back just before he died."

Stevie felt a surge of adrenaline. It was the connection between the two murders she'd been waiting for — tangible evidence Scott had been delving into Gina's death before his own murder.

"Dana, I need that journal right away. I think there might be something very important in it. Do you have it?"

"Yeah, sure, I've got it in storage with the rest of her stuff. I couldn't part with Gina's things. I guess I still can't, so I rented a storage place for it. And since the break-in, I —"

"What break-in?" Stevie interrupted, alarm raising her voice.

"The house was broken into a year ago last fall."

"When exactly?"

"It was November 23. I remember because it was the day after what would have been Gina's forty-second birthday."

Shit. A couple of months before Scott was killed. "What was taken?"

"You're scaring me, detective. Do you think someone was after the diary?"

Stevie ignored the question and repeated her earlier one. "What was taken, Dana?"

"Nothing. But drawers were pulled out, mattresses sliced open. Stuff all over the place."

"And where was the journal, in storage?"

"Yes, with the rest of her stuff."

"Look, I need you to courier it to me right away."

CHAPTER FIVE

Jovanowksi's face — hooded, red-rimmed eyes, and drooping mouth — told Stevie his visit to Shelton had been a long and frustrating one.

His bulk made the bed creak as he sat, his briefcase bouncing as he tossed it on the other side of Stevie's outstretched legs. The two of them were like caged lions, for Stevie was no happier, thanks to orders from Jade to stay in bed until the penicillin knocked the streptococcus from her body.

Thick fingers swept over Jovanowski's eyes, lingering to rub the exhaustion from them. "Shelton

PD has no idea what Walters or Scott might have been up to that could have brought harm to them. Big surprise, eh?"

Stevie nodded dolefully, already having concluded that the Shelton police force, for whatever reason, couldn't be counted on for any help. "Did they offer to let you see their case files?"

Jovanowski laughed facetiously. "They were only too happy to, except Walters's stuff has all been destroyed by now because none of her cases are outstanding."

Stevie fell into a bout of coughing. "Figures. And Scott's?"

A sardonic shake of the head. "Either misfiled or buried in some dusty storage room. They said it'd take weeks to track down. Scott's son doesn't have anything except his personal effects and what was in his safety deposit box. I only talked to him over the phone, but he's going to be here on business tomorrow and has agreed to meet with us. Are you in?"

Stevie stole a glance at the half-open bedroom door to be sure Jade wasn't hovering, then nodded. "Any other insight the department thought to share?"

Jovanowski hedged. "The chief, a guy named Bob Dales, told me Gina Walters was gay. Said she paid a visit to the department's psychologist once, and his report said she was 'maladjusted' over her sexuality, whatever that means."

"That's crap. Her lover says she was fine about it."

"Maybe that's what Dana Jeffries wants to believe."

"Maybe it's what the department wants to believe," Stevie shot back. "Maybe they damn well wanted a report to say that so they could bust her back to

43

patrol or maybe right out of the force because of these trumped-up psychological problems."

Jovanowski shrugged. "You got a point there, Tex."

Stevie held up the leather-bound journal in her hands. "I've been going through this thing all day — Gina's personal journal for the two years prior to her death."

She explained how she'd gotten hold of it, and about the break-in at Jeffries's home that was probably a cover to search for the journal and any other evidence on whatever she was working on. "There's some interesting stuff. Listen to —"

Jade clattered her way into the bedroom with a tray containing two ceramic mugs, spoons, a creamer, and a bowl of sugar, all balancing precariously.

"Thought you two could use something hot to drink."

Jovanowski took the mug of coffee like the caffeine junkie he was. Stevie scowled at the other mug, its liquid green and its smell that of dead grass and burning weeds.

"What the hell is this?"

Jade sweetly kissed Stevie's cheek, her voice syrupy. Her eyes weren't amused. "You're welcome, dear."

Stevie's forehead smoothed, her voice softer. "You know I don't like this weird shit. I'd like some coffee too."

"It's herbal tea, and it's better for you than coffee. When you're feeling better you can go back to caffeine," Jade smiled warmly.

Stevie rolled her eyes in Jovanowski's direction, but cradled the warm mug anyway, secretly enjoying the way Jade doted on her. "Want to join us, hon?"

"Sorry, I'm working on a report I need to finish before I show my face at the office in the morning."

Stevie knew her illness had put Jade behind in her work. She'd taken the morning off to stay home and look after Stevie, something Stevie knew she would have had difficulty doing if the shoe had been on the other foot. She winked affectionately at her lover as she departed.

When Stevie looked at Jovanowski again, there was a flash of envy in his eyes, and that ubiquitous melancholy that seemed to shroud his very soul. She shuddered, hoping to God she didn't have to end up alone some day — alone like him, alone the way she'd wanted to be until Jade had breezed into her life, made her realize how much more joyful life could be with someone special in it.

"Any suicidal or depressing thoughts in there?" Jovanowski asked, all business again.

"Nothing like that. In fact she seemed pretty satisfied with her life. But there is one area I'm confused about. Near the end, she keeps referring to someone by the name of J. M. Stuff like 'I'm thinking of J. M. again and yet I know I shouldn't be,' and how they need to really talk about things." She flipped the pages until she came to the right spot. "And there's a passage that says 'K. is still a problem'."

Jovanowski thought for a moment. "Any idea who the hell these people are?"

Stevie shook her head. "I'll phone Dana tonight."

"What about specific cases she was working on, anything like that?"

"Everything's pretty cryptic. She does complain about getting a lot of shitty cases." Stevie grinned knowingly. "Sounds familiar. But there's some stuff later about how much longer she can keep this investigation up—"

"What investigation?"

Stevie shrugged in frustration. "And how she knows she'll soon have to find a new career. How 'after this, I can never give my heart to policing again.' The rest of the stuff in here is pretty run-of-the-mill, everyday stuff."

Jovanowski was silent for a few minutes, rubbing his chin thoughtfully. "Wonder why she was so turned off her career all of a sudden."

Stevie shook her head in wonder. "Isn't that the question of the day."

Jovanowski affectionately patted her knee and rose. "Better let you get some rest, kid, or Jade'll be in here dragging me away. Meet me at the office at two tomorrow."

Stevie got to the office twenty minutes early, anxious to share with her partner what was perplexing her. She'd phoned Dana Jeffries earlier that morning to ask her who the mysterious initials in Gina's diary belonged to.

Jovanowski cursed after Stevie explained. "What d'ya mean she doesn't know who J. M. and K. are?" It wasn't a question so much as Jovanowski blowing off steam.

Stevie shrugged, absently stroking her cheek with the eraser tip of her pencil as she leaned back in her chair, her eyes roaming to the window. Jovanowski slumped on the edge of the desk, tapping his foot on the floor. They would often go for minutes like this,

46

both silently consumed with their own thoughts, forming more questions in their minds.

"She says she doesn't have a clue, Ted," Stevie finally answered, her dark eyes back on her partner. "Figures they're work associates."

Jovanowski's face darkened. "Did you believe her?"

Stevie was now rolling the pencil over her upper lip and staring blankly and unblinking at the snow falling past the third-floor window. "It was just over the phone. But no, I didn't believe her."

Stevie swung her gaze back to her partner, threw her pencil down. "She hesitated when I asked her — she was tense, like she wasn't quite sure how to answer."

Stevie watched the tall, wiry man with thatchlike dark hair approach them from across the room, his two-piece suit flapping with each stride. Thick glasses diminished his dark eyes until they looked like two black pebbles pressed into his pale, gaunt face, like raisins in cookie dough.

"Are you Detective Jovanowski?"

Jovanowski hopped off the desk. "Yeah. Jim Scott?"

The man smiled a row of tiny teeth. For some perverse reason she'd never been able to figure out, Stevie didn't trust people with little, pointy teeth.

"Jim, this is my partner, Detective Stephanie Houston."

A bony hand lightly shook Stevie's — too lightly — providing another reason she immediately disliked Harding Scott's son. Stevie quickly withdrew her hand. "You can call me Stevie, Jim." She forced a thin smile to soften the flatness in her voice.

"Let's go into an interview room," Jovanowski suggested, leading the way to a windowless room with a large, polished rectangular table and functional chairs.

He closed the door as Stevie and Jim Scott took seats opposite each other. "Can I get either of you a cup of coffee before we get started?"

Stevie coughed and shook her head, reluctantly remembering Jade's orders. Jim Scott declined too.

"All right, let's get started then. Why don't you tell us something about yourself first, Jim?"

"I'm not a suspect or anything like that, am I?" He smiled nervously, his golf ball–like Adam's apple bobbing in his skinny neck.

Jovanowski waved his hand dismissively. "Of course not, Jim. We just want to get to know you a little better."

He was twenty-eight years old, he told them, his little eyes squinting, as though the glasses still weren't strong enough. He was an only child and ran a computer store in a city near Shelton. He'd been close with his dad, especially since his mother had died when he was still a teenager.

Stevie's pen was poised over her notebook. "Did your father ever talk to you about his job?"

Bony shoulders shrugged before slumping in repose. "Sure, sometimes. Just general stuff."

"Did he ever talk about any cases he was working on?"

"No, never. He was really particular about not getting into details. He felt that sort of thing was really unprofessional."

Stevie nodded perfunctorily. "Did he ever give you any reason to think he was unhappy with his job?"

Jim Scott stared at his folded hands. "Since his heart attack, and since Gina Walters died, he never seemed the same about the job again."

"What do you mean?" Jovanowski demanded.

"I don't know. He didn't seem as gung-ho about it. Just a couple of months before he died, he said he wanted to retire as soon as he had his thirty years in, which would have been in a couple of years. That was so totally unlike him. I mean, he always used to talk about being a cop until they booted him out at sixty. It was his life."

Stevie thoughtfully tapped the end of her pencil on her chin. "What did your father think of Gina Walters? Did they get along?"

"Yeah, sure, they got along OK," Scott shrugged. "He never said anything bad about her."

"Did he ever talk about her death, about whether he thought it was suicide?" Jovanowski asked.

"Do you think it wasn't?" Scott asked in surprise, a mist of sweat dotting his upper lip, like morning dew.

"I didn't say that," Jovanowski answered impatiently. "What did your father think?"

"Right after it happened, he said he found it hard to believe, that he thought she would have talked to him if she'd been having problems. That's all he said about it."

An uncomfortable silence followed, and it became obvious the three could never sit down at a dinner table together.

"You said you'd bring some things from your father's safety-deposit box," Jovanowski prodded.

Scott clumsily thumped a briefcase down on the table and clicked it open. He pulled out a large, sealed manila envelope.

"My dad and I had a talk just a few weeks before he was killed." Scott drew his hand over his five o'clock shadow. "He told me he was sealing some information in an envelope in his safety-deposit box. Said it had something to do with a case, but that I was not to give it to the Shelton police if he died prematurely."

Stevie and Jovanowski briefly eyed each other.

"Did he explain?" Stevie asked.

Scott shook his head.

Jovanowski slid the envelope over and clasped his big hands protectively over it. "Why did you not give this to my department after your father was killed?"

Scott fidgeted in the seat his thin frame failed to fill. "To tell you the truth, I'd forgotten about it. I'd put it in my own safety-deposit box until now." He glanced down at his hands like a scorned child. "I'm sorry. I don't want you to think I don't want my dad's murder solved, because I do, honest."

Jovanowski stood abruptly, his body language telling Stevie he shared her natural dislike for this boy-man who appeared so ill at ease with other people. "We'll be in touch if we have any questions. Thank you for coming."

Scott stood, adjusting his cheap suit jacket. "There is one more thing, detectives." His face screwed up. "After my dad's funeral, the Shelton police — the chief, actually — asked to look through all my dad's personal stuff."

"And did they?" Stevie asked.

"Yes, except for that safety-deposit box stuff."

Jovanowski nodded, softening a bit. "Listen son, remember, it's important that our conversations remain confidential."

After showing Jim Scott out, Jovanowski came back to the interview room and dropped heavily into the chair. He fingered the envelope. "Strange little character, isn't he?"

"My thoughts exactly."

"I sure hope in hell he's trustworthy and doesn't go blabbing around Shelton about this envelope. Shall we?" He carefully opened the envelope, softly shaking its contents onto the table.

They both stared, as though afraid to touch the items.

Jovanowski licked his lips, then slowly picked up a photograph. It was a cop, his Shelton shoulder flashes visible on his uniform, his dirty blond hair graying at the temples, his square face unsmiling. There was nothing written on the back. Another photo, this one an aerial shot of some sort of mansion. Again, nothing identifying it.

Stevie picked up the last two photos, both close-ups of fingerprints. She studied them carefully, turning them over. Her eyes widened.

"Well, I'll be damned."

Jovanowski looked up. "What?"

"There's a date and an address."

"And?"

"November 24, Dana Jeffries's address. The day after the break-in. Shit, Ted. Harding Scott went in there and collected his own prints. He knew the Shelton police weren't to be trusted."

"And I'll bet he didn't care too much for whoever this joker in uniform is."

Stevie squinted at the picture, her chin jutting out confidently. "We'll find him."

"You're damned right about that." Jovanowski's eyes caught fire. "Take a look at this."

Stevie took the slip of paper from him. It was printed in large letters, the way a teacher might print on a chalkboard for kids learning the alphabet.

She felt ill as she read the words. Rage and nausea swirled heavily in her stomach. She didn't realize her fists had clenched in anger at her sides.

CHAPTER SIX

Inspector McLemore, his face expressionless, stared silently at the note between his fingers — the note that proclaimed THE ONLY GOOD DYKE IS A DEAD DYKE.

He'd patiently listened to Stevie and Jovanowski outline the evidence they had, knew that whatever was going on, they'd just scratched the surface. They weren't even remotely close to zeroing in on whoever was responsible for the murders, which, it was increasingly clear, were very likely connected. He had to agree with them there was something poisonous going on in Shelton.

"You're sure there was no mention anywhere in Shelton's reports of a hate campaign against Walters?"

Jovanowski shook his head grimly. "In fact when I interviewed the chief, and he showed me the psychologist's letter talking about Gina being maladjusted to her sexuality, he told me it wasn't a problem with her coworkers. He said it'd never come up."

"One big happy family," Stevie mumbled acidly.

McLemore slid the note back into the envelope — the envelope that had come from Scott's safety-deposit box. He knew what their next step had to be, but first he wanted to be sure in his own mind it was the only option they had.

"What about that break-in at Jeffries's house? What's the Shelton PD have to say about that?"

Jovanowski grimaced. "I had them fax me their report this morning. Nothing was taken, so they weren't too concerned."

"Did they dust for prints?"

"Of course. But they came up with diddly — so they say. Funny how Scott came up with prints, though."

"Anything on those prints?"

"No matches from CPIC, sir, and nothing from AFIS," Stevie answered. "We've asked our people to take a closer look at them."

McLemore fingered the photo of the unnamed Shelton cop. Was that Scott's way of saying those prints belonged to this mystery cop?

McLemore drummed his yellowed fingers on his desktop, his eyes granitelike. "We've got to send someone in."

Stevie and Jovanowski both nodded in unison. It was apparent to all of them that planting a cop in the

Shelton PD was the only way they were going to find evidence to link the two murders, to find the answers to the clues Scott had left behind and to get to the bottom of the strange behavior of the police department. But could they pull off such an intricate cover?

"Stevie," McLemore lined his sights on her. "I'll have to get the permission of the Ministry of the Attorney General first since Shelton is out of our jurisdiction, but you're going inside the line as soon as we can arrange it."

Jovanowski shifted uncomfortably in his seat at the words *inside the line* — the phrase cops commonly used for going undercover to investigate other cops. "Inspector, I don't think sending Stevie inside is a good idea. It sounds more like going *over the line*, if you ask me."

"What's the problem, Ted?" McLemore snapped. He didn't like to be challenged. "They already know who you are, but they don't know Stevie. And she's young enough to remember things like the Highway Traffic Act."

Jovanowski let the insult harmlessly bounce off him and sullenly chewed the inside of his cheek.

"Besides, if there is something sinister going on in that department, they're not as likely to view Stevie as a threat," McLemore continued. "She's yours and she's female. We're just lucky she was sick earlier this week and didn't make the trip to Shelton."

Jovanowski looked expectantly at Stevie, willing her to protest her new assignment.

She knew her partner wanted her to reject it, to tell their inspector that she was just as gay as Gina Walters, just as likely to be the target of the same raging homophobe who'd written the note Scott had found.

She stared back, her gaze sure, and in that instant, made up her mind.

"Let me know when it's arranged," Stevie answered evenly.

Stevie followed Jovanowski through the labyrinthine corridors on the sixth floor of police headquarters until they came to a set of large double doors. A sign indicated they were entering forensic identification services.

Stevie put one foot in front of the other, barely cognizant of where they were going. She felt a tug of emptiness inside — a sudden void since Jade's emotional withdrawal.

Upon being told the night before that Stevie would soon be sent undercover to Shelton, Jade had refused to meet Stevie's eyes and had been silent and remote the rest of the evening. Even in bed, she'd rolled as far away from Stevie as she could and had left for work before Stevie awoke. All of it an intentional retreat.

Stevie, as Jade would often point out was typical, was having a hard time identifying her feelings. She was angry, for sure. Did Jade think she wanted to be away from her, to be away from everything and everyone familiar to her? Did Jade think she enjoyed dangerous situations, for godsakes?

Distractedly, Stevie studied the textured wall as Jovanowski engaged the fingerprint technician in conversation. Angry or not, underneath it all Stevie felt panicked inside at the thought of Jade's emotional absence. She turned away and leaned against the door frame for support. Goddamn, she couldn't take Jade leaving her, couldn't take being abandoned again.

Stevie could feel sweat breaking out on her forehead and blood rushing in her ears. She was five years old again. It was the day of the funeral, the day she realized Sarah wasn't coming back. Then it was the first day she had to return to school without her. The averted looks, the stares when people thought she didn't notice, the whispers. It was all coming back to her again, every painful sequence in fast forward. The Winnie the Pooh doll that was Sarah's favorite, photographs of her — all of them gone one day when Stevie came home from school. But that wasn't even the worst of it. Oh no, that was yet to come and was much more permanent: Stevie's growing invisibility to her parents, her older brother and sister. To them, it was somehow Stevie's fault Sarah was never coming back again; it was Stevie's fault she looked just like Sarah, talked like Sarah, the Sarah who was gone forever. She had been abandoned first by her twin sister, then by the rest of her family.

Stevie squeezed her eyes tight to blink back the tears forming. *Christ.* She needed a drink. Why the hell was she doing this to herself?

"You OK, Tex?" Jovanowski whispered, suddenly concerned. "You look like you're going to puke or something."

Stevie straightened and took a deep breath. "Yeah, I'm fine."

The technician, a short Japanese man named Kubota, was pointing to a computer screen and an enhanced version of the fingerprint photos from

Scott's safety-deposit box. There were two thumb prints, and the prints of the index and middle fingers of the right hand.

He peered into the screen, his face an enigma of age, his hair jet black and cropped short. "As you can see, I've scanned them in. Nothing too unusual. The arches are somewhat tented, as you can see. But again, that's not unusual."

"Shit. Guess I was hoping for some kind of miracle," Jovanowski grumbled.

"What, like some incredibly rare pattern or some complex set of whorls with a dozen deltas?" Kubota's smile was lopsided, amusement flickering in his black eyes. "I'm afraid this isn't an episode of *Quincy, Detective.*"

He turned back to the computer, his nose practically brushing against it, his eyes straining. He shook his head faintly.

"What is it, Kubota?"

He ignored the question for a few minutes, then slowly stood. "Nothing, I guess. But I'll keep this on my hard drive, see if I can come up with anything that might be helpful."

Stevie threw the last of her TV dinner in the garbage, still irritated by Jade's message on the answering machine that she had an early evening postmortem and wouldn't be home until after midnight. Perhaps it was true. Stevie hoped so — hoped to God it wasn't some lame excuse to punish her some more.

She'd just sat down with the *Toronto Star* when the phone rang.

"Stevie, McLemore here. You're to report for duty in Shelton at 0700 hours Monday."

Stevie swallowed hard. It was already Thursday. "That soon? How'd you do it?"

"The ministry is very interested in what we've come up with. As it turns out, they've had anonymous calls for the past year about the police department being corrupt, but they've never been able to come up with as much as we have."

"But how'd you get me in so soon?"

"As luck would have it, they hired a new constable just two weeks ago, and he was to start Monday. We convinced him not to report and offered him a job here he couldn't refuse. After that, it was a piece of cake. With the ministry's blessing, we had central hiring tell them you were the only qualified candidate on their list right now that they could slide right in. They've been told you've spent the past year as a part-time constable with our department."

"What about a place to stay?"

"Taken care of. We've arranged for you to rent the apartment he was going to take. Now tomorrow I want you and Jovanowski in for a debriefing and to talk with a ministry supervisor. And one more thing. We need to falsify some ID for you immediately. We need to alter your name. What'll it be?"

Stevie fumbled for time, bit her lip. Then it came to her. "Sarah. Sarah Lauren Houston. She was my twin sister. She died when we were five."

"Excellent. See you tomorrow."

Stevie sank back in the leather recliner, clutching

the glass of bourbon in her hand. How was she going to tell Jade she'd be leaving so soon? More than that, how the hell was she ever going to make this one up to her?

She took a sip, then another and another until the glass was drained.

Stevie found it hard not to stare at the captivating woman sitting across the polished table from her. Jovanowski, looking even more bedazzled, had developed a slight stutter.

"Until you people came along, we really had nothing but a few vague, anonymous tips," she said matter-of-factly, her face divulging no excitement in a case that had been sitting on the ministry's back burner for months.

"Was it the same person who called each time?" Inspector McLemore asked her.

He'd shown not a glimmer of attraction or interest in the ministry investigator. He was so damn smooth, Stevie mused. Was the man not human?

A barely imperceptible shake of her head. "One was a letter, typed and postmarked from Shelton. Two were phone calls. It's a man's voice, nothing distinctive about it."

She was tall, about Stevie's height, and looked every inch the athlete. But not the crash-and-bang brute that Stevie was when it came to sports. Rather, she had that lithe grace that belonged to those naturally-gifted athletes who made strength, speed, and agility look so damn effortless. Probably excelled at sports like swimming and track, Stevie guessed. Her short hair had begun to prematurely silver, and she had the bluest eyes Stevie had ever seen. There was a gentleness in her high cheekboned, Nordic-looking face, but it was not to be mistaken for incompetence or apathy. Every movement, every word, was efficient, necessary, and her eyes missed nothing in front of her.

Jocelyn Travers was forty-two years old and had worked as a street cop for six years, McLemore had told them earlier when she stepped out to take a phone call. She'd spent her spare time getting her law degree, and with her background as a cop, she'd moved immediately into the ministry as a special investigator.

Stevie was relieved the woman had been a cop. So many of these government types were self-righteous and had no idea of what a cop's job entailed. But more than that, Jocelyn Travers, who insisted immediately on first names only, seemed to treat Jovanowski and Stevie as equals, as team members.

"When did these tips start?" Stevie asked, forcefully shifting her eyes to her notebook.

"Last March."

"Just after Harding Scott's death," McLemore interjected. "Any clues as to who this interested party is?"

Jocelyn shook her head. "Could be anyone. A cop, a police commissioner, a city council member, even a newspaper reporter. We tried to negotiate with him, said we would protect him and get him out of Shelton if he was in a compromising position. But he wouldn't go for it, and he didn't call again."

Jovanowski glanced warily at Stevie. "Scared him off maybe?"

Jocelyn nodded regretfully. "It was me that took

that last call, and yes, I think I pushed too hard. I blew it."

Stevie smiled at the woman's frankness, admired her calm self-reproachment. If there's anything they didn't need, it was an obnoxious government prick, and thankfully they'd been spared that.

"What did he say about the corruption?" Stevie asked.

"Just that more than half the department was corrupt. His exact word was that they'd been *bought.*" She leaned into the table and solemnly addressed Stevie and Jovanowski, pulling the half-moon reading glasses off her face. "We want to keep this investigation quiet. If it became public too early, it could have a whole town running scared. And not only that. If we went in there with all the cannons firing, I have a feeling we'd hit a brick wall. We already did background checks on all the Shelton police officers, including management. No criminal records or serious discipline activity, and financial checks came up with nothing out of the ordinary."

Stevie nodded slowly. So she wasn't just going after murderers, but dirty cops as well. It was now her job to find out if there was a connection between the murders and the graft. "You'll be in regular contact with Ted while I'm inside?"

Jocelyn smiled, confidence brimming in her eyes. "I'll be extremely interested in your daily activities. Ted and I will be talking every day."

Stevie caught the grin forming at the corners of Jovanowski's mouth. *Poor guy.*

Jocelyn's smile faded, her face intense once again. "Stevie, since you're basically on your own with this, it's very important that you talk to us every step of the way. The minute you find out anything concrete, or if you have any hint that they're on to you, we're pulling you out."

McLemore stared hard at Stevie as if to drive the point home.

Stevie smiled. She could handle this.

CHAPTER SEVEN

Stevie tried to stretch in the passenger seat of the police cruiser, then quickly stopped herself as the cotton fabric of her light-blue uniform shirt tightened around her chest. The uniform had been thrown together for her — the shirt too small, the pants too baggy. At least the heavy nylon coat fit.

Her sergeant, who had chosen to accompany her on her first shift for the Shelton Police Department, wheeled the car into the snowy parking lot of a doughnut shop.

"Why don't you get us a coupla coffees." His

suggestion was a barely-concealed order. There was no forthcoming offer of coins or bills either.

Stevie frowned as she exited the car and carefully maneuvered her away across the slick pavement. She was being treated no better than a cadet. But she'd have to hold her temper, she reminded herself. As hard as it was going to be, she'd need to act like an inexperienced constable still fresh enough out of police college — one who was content just to wear a uniform and carry a badge. She'd be a nonentity, a nonthreat.

Stevie waited in line, trying to ignore the whispers, the stares — some curious, some downright unfriendly. She'd almost forgotten how magnetic a uniform was, how much attention it attracted.

Unfortunately, the uniform was more often like horseshit than honey, she smiled to herself as her first fly buzzed up to her, two of his friends following.

"Looks like another girlie cop in town," the man snorted, his friends chortling behind him.

Stevie turned to face him, crossing her arms over her chest and rocking confidently on her heels. Her gnat was about two inches shorter than her and probably twenty pounds lighter, his smile crooked and toothless, his face too bony and worn for such a young man.

She watched silently, unblinking as he stepped closer. His breath was thick with the stench of stale coffee and cigarettes.

"Hey, I know how come girls wanna be cops. They wanna carry a gun 'cause they don't got one-a these." He grinned and grabbed his crotch as his friends howled their approval.

Contempt, then amusement, flared in Stevie's eyes as her mind bubbled with all sorts of humiliating retorts and verbal punishment for this asshole. Her wink was wicked, her voice icy. "You're right. If I had what you had," she nodded toward his midsection, "I wouldn't need to carry a pistol. I'd need a bloody cannon."

Chuckles and guffaws erupted. Stevie quickly scooped up her coffees and left, not wanting a bigger scene.

"What the hell took you so long?" her sergeant grumbled, his balding head wrinkled in irritation.

"Oh, just some locals wanting to introduce themselves to me. At least one of them seemed a little surprised to see a woman in uniform."

The sergeant, Larry Edgar, mumbled and maneuvered the car out of the lot, juggling the wheel and his coffee.

"There's one other woman constable besides me, right?"

"Yeah. Jackson."

Stevie sipped her lukewarm coffee, warming to the idea of gauging Edgar's reaction to women cops. "There haven't been many in the past, I take it."

He shrugged narrow shoulders. "Jackson's been here a year, though how much longer . . ."

"What do you mean?"

Another evasive shrug. "Doesn't seem to be fitting in all that well."

Stevie nodded, making a mental note to get to know this Jackson woman. "Anyone else before her?"

Edgar glanced sideways at her, his voice strangely devoid of emotion. "Just one other. She was here quite a few years but couldn't hack it either. Shot herself in the head."

Stevie stared at him, trying her best to look surprised. "What happened?"

Edgar shook his head. "Nothing really. Just went out to an empty field and shot herself with her service revolver."

"Why would she do that?" Stevie pressed. "Wouldn't she go for help or something?"

"Hmph! Help?" Edgar's voice rose spitefully. "What kind of help is there for being queer?"

Stevie's eyes widened in mock naïveté. She nodded in conspiratorial judgment, hating every second of it. She wondered how many others on the force were just as unapologetically homophobic as Edgar. She'd drop the subject for now, for she knew she might as well just stick a rainbow sign on her back as make some right-wing proclamation about nothing being wrong with gays.

As the afternoon dimmed and their shift wound down, Edgar pulled into a downtown parking lot, now empty of cars, and pulled out his notebook to do some paperwork.

Stevie ignored Edgar, who wasn't much for conversation anyway, and grabbed a map of the city from the glove box. She worked on memorizing the street names and sectors — the main routes first, the quickest routes to the hospital, the city's bars and nightclubs. But her mind felt like a sieve, her concentration shifting like sand. Finally, she could no longer avoid the pull of Jade and the clenching of her heart.

Jade had taken it pretty hard when Stevie said they shouldn't see each other weekends while she was undercover. They couldn't risk her cover being blown, or anyone in Shelton suspecting Stevie was gay. After that discussion, they hadn't talked much all weekend — their truce a silent one.

Stevie hadn't admitted it to Jade, or to anyone, but it made her sick to have her career come between them like this. Policing, and her relationship with Jade, were the two things Stevie loved most in her life. Yet, at times like this, the two couldn't seem to coexist, their incompatiblity pushing and pulling her in different directions. She could only hope it didn't have to come to a choice some day, knowing either scenario would leave her with a void.

Stevie gazed at the dusky sky. Unabashedly, she knew she would choose Jade, if it came to that.

"Hey, look at that," she said to Edgar, squinting through the murky light at a couple embracing and kissing, the male leaning against the blackened brick wall in an alley across the street, the woman pushing her rakish body into him.

Edgar grunted, uninterested. Stevie, eager for something to do, watched with growing interest. The woman pawed at the man's crotch, their kissing more intense. Then her hand slid into his front pocket and withdrew what looked like bills.

Stevie reached for the door handle. Edgar reached for her.

"What do you think you're doing?"

"It looks like something's going down. Solicitation or at least indecent acts in a public place." Stevie consciously swallowed her confidence. "Wouldn't you say, sir?"

Edgar shook his head. "That's just Kelly Bronskill. She's a hooker and a druggie."

"Shouldn't we charge them? She's obviously about to turn a trick."

"Just hold it there, Houston. Leave her alone."

"Why?" Stevie tried not to sound startled, even though she was. She was a cop about to turn her back on a criminal offense right before her eyes.

Edgar shrugged. "We leave her be. She informs for us sometimes."

Stevie yanked up her jeans, then neatly folded her dark wool uniform pants, setting them on a shelf in her locker.

"Hi."

Stevie hadn't noticed the stocky young woman leaning against the door frame, watching her. Stevie nodded to the stranger in uniform.

"I'm Sue Jackson." The officer stepped closer and offered her hand.

Stevie shook it, their grips equally firm. "Sarah Houston."

"Yeah, I know." She smiled, her gray eyes brightening to near-blue, freckles barely visible, her wavy blond hair cropped short. "Welcome aboard."

"Thank you," Stevie smiled back, her gaydar needle jumping off the scale.

"Would you like to go out for coffee some time, say, tomorrow night after your shift?"

Stevie nodded casually, secretly relieved an emotional ally was in sight. "That'd be great."

"Didn't take you long, Jackson." The voice — a man's — drifted down the hallway, the tone caustic. "Exhausted your local supply of women already?"

Stevie stepped out in time to see the tall, square-shouldered, uniformed man swaggering away. She couldn't see his face, but he had a full head of dull blond hair flecked with gray.

Jackson angrily pushed past Stevie. "Hey, Mercer, I had to since your wife keeps telling me no."

The man swung around, his face clenched and red, his eyes stony, full of hate. Then his body slackened, his mouth drooping into a smirk before he turned.

Stevie froze. It was him. The cop in the photo they'd been given by Harding Scott's son. She'd found the sonofabitch.

"Who was that?" Stevie asked, her voice thick and even.

"Kent Mercer. He's one of the veterans." Jackson shook her head and stormed off.

CHAPTER EIGHT

Stevie sat at the corner table, her eyes riveted on the door. She watched it swing open, felt the draft of cold air usher Sue Jackson in.

They shook hands again, a little stiffly on Stevie's part. She felt uncomfortable around the young cop, who had done or said nothing to cause this mild case of effrontery. Maybe it was just the way she had silently watched her dress in the locker room yesterday. Or maybe it was the unspoken invitation that seemed to linger in her smile.

Stevie sat back down and mentally shrugged it off.

She could trust no one in Shelton right now, especially anyone connected with the police department, whether they deserved such cynicism or not.

Gray eyes settled over Stevie like a cool mist, all-encompassing. "It's nice to finally have another woman on staff."

"It mustn't have been easy the past, what, year or so that you've been on?"

Jackson nodded, her smile fleeting, her eyes faltering for a moment. "They're bastards, most of them."

Stevie exhaled, caught between wanting to offer encouragement and keeping an objective distance. "I get the sense at least some of them don't have much use for women in this business. Is this your first policing job?"

Jackson nodded. "You?"

Stevie eagerly smiled back and launched into her rehearsed past. "Well, my first real job. I spent a year as a part-time officer in Toronto, and I was a special constable before that — you know, court security and that type of thing. But I wanted the real thing."

Jackson's smile was wry. "It's probably best you don't plan on staying here long. I'm getting out the first chance I can land another policing job somewhere else. You should too."

"That bad, eh?"

"Hell, the last woman in this hellhole put a gun to her head." She shook her head emphatically. "I'm sure they'd love to drive me to that too."

A waitress stopped in front of their table, her tapping foot impatient, her mouth sculpting a wad of gum. "What'll you girls have?"

"Coffee?" Stevie looked at Jackson, then nodded to

the waitress, who took the order and left. "Why do they hate you so much?" Stevie asked.

Jackson leaned back against the cheap maple chair, her arms protectively crossed over her chest, her eyes steeled for any forthcoming challenges — imagined or real. "I guess it's not too hard to figure out after you saw that exchange outside the locker room. I happen to prefer women in my bed."

Stevie nodded impassively, resisting the urge to tell this woman she knew exactly how she felt. But it was too risky to reach out to this stranger whose agenda was still unknown — if indeed there was an agenda, and for the moment at least, Stevie had to assume everyone here had one.

Jackson waited — for an admission perhaps — boldly holding Stevie's gaze. "Anyway, it's just another piece of ammunition for them to fling at me."

"Has anyone ever threatened you because of it?" Stevie asked, her voice low and impervious to the urgent curiosity she felt. If homophobia had caused Gina Walters's death, then surely Sue Jackson was just as much at risk.

Jackson shook her head. "Nah, nothing like that. They just try to make it hell for me, like they did the woman detective who shot herself."

"Did you know her?"

"No, I'm not from here and she's been dead a few years. But I heard they gave her a hard time too because she was gay."

Their coffees arrived and Stevie quickly dumped cream and sugar in hers. She stirred rapidly and was mildly aware of her body stiffening.

"Something wrong?" Jackson's eyes were challenging, curious again.

Stevie shook her head. "That Kent Mercer sure seems like a homophobic jerk. He always give you a hard time?"

"Enough of the time, yeah. But I just make some comment about his wife, and he shuts up."

"What do you mean?" Stevie asked.

Jackson smiled naughtily and leaned forward, cradling the cup of black coffee in her beefy hand. "The rumor is that his wife Jan had an affair with Gina Walters — you know, the cop who shot herself."

Stevie exhaled softly, keeping her surprise at this new piece of information under wraps. If the affair were true, why hadn't Dana Jeffries mentioned it? Unless, of course, she had no idea.

Jackson settled back in her chair. "I suspect Mercer's had a thing up his ass about homosexuality because of it. If it's true, of course."

"Are the Mercers still together?"

"Apparently." Jackson set her cup down, her eyes gliding favorably over Stevie. "Would you like to, you know, go out for a drink or dinner sometime?"

Stevie smiled to herself and took a sip of the syrupy coffee. Was this a test of her own preference, or did this woman have a little crush on her? Stevie decided to meet the challenge head on.

"Are you asking me for a date?"

Jackson's resolve crumbled a bit, as she obviously considered whether to backtrack or plow ahead. She hesitated, her eyes dropping to the table for an instant, her hands nervously toying with her cup. Then her mouth tightened. "Yeah, I am."

Stevie wanted to applaud the woman's guts, throwing the ball back in her court like that. "I'm sorry. But, friends?"

Jackson winked, braver by the second. "Sure. But don't expect me to give up on the other yet."

Stevie took the bus to Dana Jeffries's house, not willing to take a chance by driving there with her rented car. There was no reason for anyone to be suspicious of her and she had no reason to believe she was being followed. But still, if she was being followed, she'd be an easier target in a car, and she had been warned to take precautions.

Immediate surprise registered on Dana Jeffries's face as she opened the door to a plainclothes Stevie.

"Detective Houston — what are you doing in Shelton?"

Stevie stood on the porch, shivering. "Can I come in?"

Jeffries smiled in embarrassment at her momentary lack of manners. "Of course. Please do."

Stevie stepped around cardboard boxes, remembering Jeffries had been planning to move to Toronto. She pulled off her snowy boots and hung her coat on a nearby peg.

"I've got tea brewing. C'mon into the kitchen."

Stevie followed, stepping neatly over more boxes, and took a seat at the kitchen table.

"Sorry I didn't let you know I was coming," Stevie explained. "But I'm working undercover here now."

Jeffries's eyebrows twitched as she leaned against the kitchen counter, kettle boiling. "Not as a police officer I hope?"

Stevie nodded gravely. "And that's not to leave this room."

Jeffries's face grew darker, her eyes widening with concern. "Please don't end up like Gina."

"Believe me, I certainly don't plan to. But we felt it was the only way to find whoever killed Gina and Harding."

Jeffries's voice was nearly inaudible. "Then you think it was someone with the police department?"

Stevie barely shrugged, lacing her fingers together on the table. "I'm not sure. But I think some people in the department at least know who did and may be covering for the murderer."

Tears began pooling in Jeffries's eyes, the color quickly draining from her face, and she turned away to fuss with the kettle. Her voice cracked when she spoke. "I can't believe they would do that to Gina, after everything she gave to that job."

Stevie tried to backpedal, realizing her mistake in revealing too much. She didn't need Dana Jeffries's emotions taking over and causing her to do something stupid, just as they were getting close. "Look, we're not sure what's happened here. All we know is that something is not right with the Shelton Police Department."

Jeffries poured tea, handing a steaming mug to Stevie, and sat down across from her.

"No one must know I'm here," Stevie said, her resolute brown eyes reinforcing the severity of her voice.

"How can I help you?"

Stevie swallowed a warm mouthful. "I asked you before who J. M. was in Gina's diary, and you said you didn't know." Stevie swallowed some tea again to quench the dryness in her mouth. She dreaded what was next and her voice was even as she said, "Could it stand for Jan Mercer?"

Jeffries's hands began to tremble. Her bottom lip twitched ever so slightly, a fresh layer of pain bubbling to the surface. "Perhaps," she answered faintly.

Stevie took a deep breath, let it out slowly while settling back and squaring her shoulders. There was no easy way to say it. "Dana, was Gina having an affair with Jan Mercer?"

Jeffries set her cup down with a loud clink, tea sloshing over the rim. Her eyes filled again, tears brimming over. "I, I don't know."

Stevie reached for her hand. "Please, it's important."

A minute, maybe two, ticked by on the large, round kitchen clock "All right, yes." Jeffries roughly wiped the tears from her cheek with the back of her hand. "I'd confronted her just the day before she was killed." Her lips trembled like a hurt child's. "She didn't even try to deny it."

Stevie tried to wall herself from the pain before her, tried hard not to feel empathy for this betrayed woman. Objectivity was sometimes frustratingly elusive, but necessary. "I'm sorry, but I'm glad you were honest with me. Do you know Kent Mercer very well?"

Jeffries shook her head. "I'd only met him a couple of times."

"Did Gina ever talk about him?"

Jeffries's composure began to return, the years having somewhat smoothed the pain of her lover's infidelity, the way rainfall dulls jagged rock to a polished surface. It was no doubt raining again in

Jeffries's heart, but not pouring. "They didn't get along. I guess it's no wonder."

"Did Gina ever feel he was a real threat to her?"

"I don't know, she never said. The whole thing only came out in the open between us right before she died. We hadn't had time to work through it. In fact, I don't even know how serious the affair was or how long it had gone on."

Stevie concentrated on her cup as she thought. "In her diary, Gina wrote 'K. is a problem.' Do you have any idea if Kent Mercer was giving her a hard time or stalking her or anything like that?"

Jeffries's eyes moved as she concentrated. "I don't know. But just before she died, there were times where she'd go rushing to the window when she heard a car go by. One time I looked too, and it was a Shelton police car."

"And that made her nervous?"

"I don't know about nervous. But uncomfortable for sure."

"She never talked about it?"

Jeffries shook her head regretfully. "Maybe it was just Mercer trying to tell her he was on to them."

Stevie thanked her and pulled her coat and boots on, wishing Jeffries had been up front with her from the beginning. What else had she held back?

"Detective" — Jeffries paused at the door, fresh urgency in her voice, the door open to the cold — "whatever you may think of Gina, she did love me. In spite of her . . . infidelity, we had a very good relationship."

Stevie couldn't resist. "Why didn't you tell me about the affair before?"

Jeffries stared at the floor, unblinking, as though she'd been scolded. "I guess I thought if you knew that about Gina, you wouldn't work as hard at solving this . . . that you would think that's what made her commit suicide."

Stevie smiled thinly, amazed by the things people said and imagined. It was her job to solve this case, no matter what she thought of Gina Walters. Still, she understood Dana Jeffries's need to be loyal to the memory of her lover.

Every bump, every nauseating breath of diesel fumes irritated Stevie on the ride back to her apartment. She liked Dana Jeffries, had privately felt sorry for her — a woman whose lesbian lover is murdered, yet her death is branded a suicide by everyone in town. And the only person who believes her and is in a position to do something about it ends up murdered himself.

Stevie shook her head at her own reflection in the window, disturbed by a new thought. Confirmation of Gina's infidelity now meant Dana Jeffries was a suspect. Could she have been so distraught over the affair that she conspired with Kent Mercer to kill her lover? Stevie stared into the darkness, not liking the taste of her hypothesis. If that were so, then why would Dana Jeffries have approached Jade about reviewing the autopsy if she'd had a hand in Gina's death?

* * * * *

The impatience in Jovanowski's voice was loud and clear as Stevie told him over the phone what she'd found out. He was even quicker than Stevie to name Jeffries a suspect.

"Maybe it's all a cover, her appearing so cooperative and wanting to find out what really happened to Walters. Maybe she wants Mercer to go down for all of it."

Stevie thought for a moment. "After all these years though? Nah, I mean, the whole investigation was dead. There was no need for her to start things up again when no one was even suspicious of her."

Jovanowski was silent with his own thoughts. "Well, we've got a hell of a lot more on Mercer than we do on Jeffries. It was his photo in Harding Scott's safety-deposit box, and if those were his prints all over that house after the break-in . . . You've got to get into Mercer's personnel files for his prints, if they have them there."

"I will, first chance I get. Hey, is Jade OK?"

"I've been checking in on her every day. Why?"

Stevie bit the inside of her cheek, wishing she had someone she could talk to about how her career was affecting her relationship with Jade. But it was no use. Other cops would just say that wives don't understand what being a cop is all about, and outsiders would think Stevie was just being pigheaded and uncompromising.

"I just think she's worried about me here," Stevie offered ambiguously.

"She'll be fine. Jade's a tough girl. Why don't you give her a call right now and tell her you're OK?"

"I will." Stevie's smile mushroomed into a grin.

"Hey, have you managed to get a date yet with Jocelyn?"

Stevie could hear Jovanowski breathing and imagined his cheeks blushing, a sheepish look in his eyes.

"Why would I be trying to get a date with her?"

Stevie chuckled. "Because she's gorgeous and she doesn't wear a wedding ring. And besides, I saw the way you were looking at her."

"And you only noticed her for my benefit, right, Tex?"

"Of course," Stevie laughed. "I'm married, remember? So, do you have a date yet or what?"

"Lay off, Houston." His gruff reply was not truly meant to scold.

CHAPTER NINE

Stevie slowed her pace, reminding herself she was walking the beat, not dashing off to the corner store. It'd been a while since she'd worked as a uniformed cop and she'd had to go through the same exercise patrolling again in a marked cruiser, remembering that taking it slow meant she could observe more. Though her real purpose in Shelton was to catch a murderer, the people in this city had a right to expect her to serve and protect them as a street cop.

She lingered on the downtown sidewalk, watched her breath swirl in a cloud before it dissipated under the glare of the streetlight. It was nearing midnight, and she pulled another storefront door to make sure it was locked. She walked on, snow crunching underfoot, blisters from her new boots grating with every step.

Stevie paused in front of the Bluebird Café, one of the few all-nighters in town, and considered whether to buy a coffee or drink the lukewarm sludge back at the office. She squinted past her pale reflection in the glass. Inside, seated at a booth with two others, was the hooker from the other day.

Her eyes remained glued on the young prostitute until the group, startled, looked up to see a uniformed cop staring at them through the window.

Stevie suddenly had an idea, and forcefully pulled on the door and strode purposefully to the booth. *Time to meet Kelly Bronskill,* she smiled to herself.

"There you are, you little shit." Stevie's eyes glared dark and uncompromising as she touched the collar of the seated woman's coat. "You're coming with me."

"What the fuck are you talking about?" the hooker protested loudly, her green eyes bloodshot, her pupils mismatched, her eyelids lazy.

"I'm talking about a warrant for your arrest. So get your shit and come with me."

"Fuck that!" she screeched, her friends silent but shooting nervous glances at one another.

Stevie tugged on the young woman's collar, indicating she meant business, and nudged her along the slippery floor in front of her, her hand viselike around a bony arm. Outside, Stevie backed her up against the building, getting an earful in return.

"All right, now shut up and listen to me," Stevie breathed, her face just inches from Kelly Bronskill's.

"You're not under arrest, but you're going to come with me to my police car around the corner."

The woman reluctantly did as Stevie ordered, mumbling incoherently as Stevie prodded her along. Stevie opened the passenger door for her and watched her clumsily seat herself, her arms hugging her chest to keep warm.

Stevie started the car, letting it idle while the heater whined to life. "Look, Kelly, I was just doing you a favor in there. And I expect one in return."

The woman glanced at Stevie, her chin drooped in a pout. "Some fucking favor."

"Look, I know you're an informant for us. It wouldn't do you any good for your friends to think you're on good terms with the Shelton police, now would it? A little act like that once in a while and they'll think you're still one of them."

Her defiant jaw slackened as she seemed to consider what Stevie told her. But it was too much for her jumbled mind to comprehend. "Fuck you. Who the hell are you, anyway?"

Stevie sighed irritably, momentarily doubting her plan. What the hell, she'd gone this far.

"I'm new here, Kelly. I'm Constable Sarah Houston, and I just want to know what it is you inform about for our department."

"Ask your fucking department."

Stevie leaned over the computerized console, her jaw set, her eyes glinting with the knowledge that she'd already won this battle, so there was no point in her opponent even trying to fight. She loved how she could switch this persona on and off so easily. She was made to be a cop.

Stevie surveyed the shivering woman beside her,

figured she'd be pretty if she weren't so malnourished and strung out. *Probably a real knockout at one time.* "I'm not going to ask my department because you're going to tell me," Stevie said icily.

The woman shifted in her seat, her eyes searching for the door handle. "It's no big deal," she said so quietly Stevie could hardly hear her. "I just tell them who's selling drugs and stuff."

"Tell who? Who do you deal with on the force?" More important, Stevie was dying to know, was why Kelly Bronskill was so protected when small-time street informants were a dime a dozen.

She looked at Stevie with eyes that wouldn't focus. Her mouth moved soundlessly, then stopped. "Just let me outta here, OK? I gotta go."

"Fine. But listen to me, Kelly. You and I are going to become friends. Got that?"

Stevie closed the door, quickly scampered to the desk, and turned the computer on. It was 3:00 A.M., and fortunately the station house was pretty much empty.

Sweat beaded down her sides, her fingers slick on the keys, her temples throbbing. She glanced at the door, her watch, back at the computer screen. Seconds later, she found the icon indicating Kent Mercer's personnel folder and clicked on it.

She hit the print button, glancing only briefly at the information on the screen while waiting for the printer. She scrolled down until she came to Mercer's fingerprints, and again hit the print button. It was common for police departments to fingerprint their own officers and keep them on file. They could then compare their prints to those found at a crime scene in case the responding officers had contaminated the scene. And before a potential officer was hired, his or her prints had to be screened to be sure the candidate didn't have a criminal background.

Stevie scooped the sheets off the printer and switched the computer off. The door abruptly swung open, and Sergeant Larry Edgar stepped in, arms lazily crossed over his chest.

"What are you doing in here, Houston?"

Stevie froze, her mouth a desert. "Just catching up on some paperwork, sir."

He frowned his disbelief. "You're supposed to be on the street. You come in here to do paperwork, and I wanna know about it. Now get out there."

"Yes, sir."

Stevie kept the papers stuffed in her coat while she finished her shift. She was exhausted by shift's end, the early morning ending busily with a break-in and a domestic dispute.

At her apartment, Stevie flattened the wrinkles from the papers and took a sip of bourbon, the sunshine and snow outside brightening the room far too much for her tired eyes.

She already knew by heart the information in Kent Mercer's file — Jocelyn Travers had seen to that. She knew he was forty-four and had been a constable with the Shelton police force for nineteen years. Married to Jan for twelve of those years, no children. No commendations for heroism, but nothing noteworthy in the discipline department either. An unremarkable career so far. Stevie found it a bit odd that he had never been promoted nor, as his files indicated, had he ever even tried for a promotion. He had not been singled out for any special training courses nor any special duties. Had he simply not been willing to go along with the political games in the office, or was there a more sinister reason for his stagnant career?

Stevie knew there were plenty of cops who liked it on the street, had no desire for anything more. The idea was foreign to her, for competing and achieving goals were what made her thrive. But what made a guy like Mercer watch officers with less seniority and experience climb over him?

The phone rang. It was the police chief's secretary, telling her that Chief Bob Dales wanted to see her right away. It was an order, not an option.

Stevie had only met Dales in passing during the few days she'd been in Shelton. She looked forward to the unexpected meeting, to see what kind of man ran such a messed-up police force. But first, she'd courier Mercer's prints to Jovanowski.

Stevie sat down in the chief's empty office, as she'd been directed to by the curt, unsmiling secretary.

His desk was plain, devoid of personal items but for one framed photo. Papers were neatly stacked in trays. She leaned over, peeking at the photo. It was of a woman — probably late thirties — and two small children, all of them smiling, all of them blond and attractive. The perfect family.

The door clicked softly open, then closed again. Stevie rose, but Chief Bob Dales walked silently past her to his desk without even acknowledging her. He folded his long body into his chair, ripped the stylish glasses from his face, and tossed them on his desk before nodding tersely at Stevie to sit down. Even with his face set in a scowl, Stevie could see that Dales was a good looking man — dark curly hair sprinkled with gray, his skin smooth, his frame sturdy. He was still a young man, probably about forty, Stevie guessed.

"Constable Houston, I won't beat around the bush here or waste our time with useless pleasantries."

Stevie was too numb from exhaustion to react to his bluntness, not having been to bed yet. Still, she'd expected some kind of little welcoming speech or a get-to-know-you interrogation cloaked in friendly conversation.

"What were you doing looking through personnel files last night?"

The numbness quickly drained from Stevie's body, a prickling sensation taking its place. She could handle computers, but was no techno-wizard. Did the computer keep a record of when files were accessed? If that were the case, was the chief just playing a game with her to see if she'd fess up that it had been her? Or had Sergeant Edgar figured out what she'd been doing and squealed to the chief?

Knowing there was no way out of the trap, Stevie cleared her throat and spoke calmly.

"I was just trying to get to know who the rest of my coworkers are. I've met so few of —"

"Those files are private. And from now on we're locking them with access only through a certain password. Just stick to your patrolling duties, Houston. Is that clear?"

"Yes, sir."

"Fine. Goodbye then."

He put his glasses back on and took a stack of papers from his desk drawer, their meeting obviously over. Stevie excused herself to his silence, not quite sure what to think of Dales's behavior. But her palms itched from the experience. She did not like the man and only hoped he bought her story.

On the way home, Stevie stopped at a phone booth, as she always did when she called Jovanowski. She didn't want anyone getting hold of her phone records and penetrating her cover. She told him about her meeting with Chief Dales, told him what a prick Dales was.

Jovanowksi laughed. "You didn't like me either when you first started working in homicide."

Stevie smiled at the memory of her first few weeks working with Jovanowski, then shook her head, her mouth curling into a frown. "He's not just a pompous jerk, Ted. I don't get a good feeling about this guy at all."

"All right. I'll see what I can find out about him, and Morcor's prints too."

Stevie pulled the toque tighter around her ears. It was cold, even though she was sweating. She slowed to a walk, silently admonishing herself for having got out of shape the past few months as a thousand needles pricked her lungs. She was naturally strong and had no trouble maintaining her weight at around a hundred and sixty-five pounds, so she too readily settled for any excuse that kept her from working out and couldn't resist that triple ice-cream cone or those ketchup-soaked spicy fries.

She crossed the street. It was then she noticed the Shelton police cruiser, headlights off, idling at the curb half a block away. Stevie resumed jogging, wishing she could have even just one night of not thinking about this case, about the Shelton police force.

She couldn't see the car but could hear the tires slowly crunching snow as it inched along behind her, keeping a distance of a few hundred feet.

Fuck! What were they doing, following her for crissakes? She didn't need this shit, she swore to herself, more angry than scared. Maybe that was the whole point of it — someone, *Mercer, maybe* — was trying to scare her. She slowed again, then stopped abruptly. She'd confront the fucker, that's what she'd do.

Stevie turned around, and headlights came to life, suddenly blinding her. She stalked toward the car, then began running toward it.

The car abruptly accelerated as it U-turned, kicking up a cloud of snow behind it as it sped off. Stevie cursed again. The snow had obscured the number and plate before the car disappeared into the darkness.

CHAPTER TEN

Stevie rubbed her tired eyes and hovered just inside the door of the women's locker room at the Shelton police station. She was in no mood for the twelve-hour day shift that lay ahead.

The night had been a restless one; sleep was meager and hadn't come easily. Once, staring groggily out the window, she thought she saw a cop car again creeping slowly past. It irritated her that she was being watched. Was it just her coworkers being nosy about the newest cop in town? Or were they keeping her under surveillance?

Sue Jackson, just finishing her night shift, plucked the clip from her pistol.

"Hi," Stevie said, joining Jackson at her locker. "How was the night shift?"

"Nice and quiet for a change."

Stevie nodded sharply. *Quiet enough for someone to keep an eye on me all night?*

"Oh, Sarah. I heard they're pulling Mercer off my shift." Her grin exuded relief. "Bad news is, you get to have him on yours."

Stevie shrugged to herself. *Bring the bastard on.* She could handle whatever he wanted to dish out.

Jackson lined her gun sight on the far wall, squinting in concentration. "Goddamn thing seems to be off. Want to come out target shooting with me some time?"

Stevie shrugged. What the hell. Target shooting was fun, and it'd been months since she'd done it. Besides, Jackson couldn't misconstrue something work-related as a date. "Sure. The department have a range somewhere?"

Jackson smirked. "This place? No way, too cheap. Some of the guys've got some sweet deal with Bradley Alsop, but no such luck for the rest of us."

Stevie leaned against a locker, fingers hooked around her belt loops, the picture of nonchalance. "Who's Bradley Alsop?"

"Rich dude in town. Actually, he owns half the bloody city." Her tone was bitter. "Lives in a big mansion on about a hundred acres just outside of town. Has both an indoor and an outdoor range — so I've heard."

"So what's this deal some of the guys have?"

Jackson stowed her gun in her locker, her back

momentarily to Stevie. "Not that they'd confide in me, mind you. But some of them are pretty thick with Alsop. They go shooting there, hang out with him, and he contributes nicely to our Christmas party."

Stevie distractedly massaged her temple. She'd never heard of such a partnership between a large segment of a police force and a private citizen. Collaborations like that were usually frowned upon because of the potential for abuse and favoritism. Did the Shelton brass know about this? Surely they must, if Sue Jackson was aware of it. And who was this Bradley Alsop, and why was he such a cop groupie? Could this be who owned more than half the cops in Shelton, if Jocelyn Travers's anonymous tipper was right? What was he getting in return for providing a firing range and contributing to the Christmas party?

Stevie kept her questions to herself, unwilling to trust anyone right now. She opened her locker, stared blurrily at nothing as she felt an invisible weight on her shoulders. There were times, like right now, when her isolation felt overwhelming. She was basically on her own, and not only looking for a cop killer, but, thanks to the government sticking their two cents in, she was supposed to be unraveling a corrupt police department too. What the hell did they think she was, for crissakes, the Bionic Woman?

She removed her uniform from the shelf and slammed the locker door shut, angry at Jocelyn Travers, angry at Ted Jovanowski and Inspector Jack McLemore. It was all fine for them; none of them had their ass on the line. *Damn.* She should be at her Sackville Street brownstone right now, sharing a morning cup of coffee with Jade and fighting over the sports section of the newspaper.

* * * * *

Stevie slowly maneuvered the patrol car along the tree-lined, winding road, squinting at passing address numbers. Another curve, another lavish home. She again double-checked the address that she'd written on the scrap of paper balled up in her hand, knew the house should be the next one on the left. At first, only snatches of the house, like pieces of a jigsaw puzzle, were visible between thick oak branches. Then she mentally froze at the unobstructed sight of the mansion belonging to Bradley Alsop, her body impulsively stiffening. *Goddamn!* It was the house in the photo from Harding Scott's collection, she was sure of it. The picture was an aerial view and had been taken in summer, but she was willing to bet her new salary it was the same place. An eight-foot-high wrought-iron fence enclosed the well-tended grounds, the large colonial house stately but innocuous with its ivy-coated, shuttered exterior. A couple of huge, aluminum-sided warehouse buildings stood in back, though there were no signs proclaiming what sort of business operated here.

The double gate to the cobblestone drive was open, but Stevie didn't dare drive in, much as her curiosity tempted her to. A man in thick gray overalls and a hard hat fussed with a snowblower. He turned awkwardly and waved at the sight of the patrol car. Stevie ignored the friendly gesture, figuring the groundskeeper had mistaken her for one of Alsop's buddies on the force. Obviously cop cars were a regular sight around this place.

Another man, this one tall and well built, wearing a trench coat, his hair a brush cut, emerged from the garage, visoring his eyes with his left hand to study the passing police car and its driver. Probably wondering why it wasn't stopping in, Stevie guessed, a spark of anxiety in her gut. Perhaps she'd been hasty in getting so close to the place in broad daylight. She sped off.

Stevie took a bus to the roadhouse restaurant, making sure she was the last one on and that no one followed her as she exited. It took a minute before she spotted Jovanowski and Jocelyn Travers in the darkened dining area. Good, she thought. They'd chosen a table in a corner where they could watch the door at the same time.

Jovanowski brightened at seeing Stevie, a wide-toothed grin on his face. They shook hands all around.

"We haven't ordered any food yet, but we did order you a beer," Jocelyn smiled warmly. "Ted said you'd be ready for a brew after working a twelve-hour shift."

Stevie nodded enthusiastically and winked. "I'd say a brew is a good start." With that, a thick frosty mug was thumped down in front of her, and Stevie drank appreciatively.

"So," Jocelyn smiled again. "How are you adapting to being a uniformed constable again?"

Stevie shrugged. "I'd forgotten how tough it can be sometimes." She shook her head, her smile self-deprecating. "I have to admit, though, it is kind of fun bouncing the misbehaving drunks out of the bars."

Jocelyn and Jovanowski nodded in unison. They understood that sense of immediate justice a cop felt in getting into a little dustup with someone deserving of being taken down a peg or two. There was courtroom justice, there was street justice, and there was cop justice.

They sipped their drinks, ordered cheeseburgers and fries, and swapped old war stories. Stevie noted the casual dress of Jovanowski and Jocelyn — jeans and sweatshirts — noticed how comfortable they seemed to be with each other. She couldn't help but wonder with amusement if they were dating.

"So," Jocelyn gently pressed, her fierce blue eyes belying her patient exterior. "Have you hit on anything yet?"

Stevie finished chewing a ketchuped fry, her earlier petulance having vanished at the sight of the two. Their presence and their camaraderie made her realize how lonely she'd become. Just a few hours ago she'd been ready to tell Jocelyn and the government where to stick it, but seeing that mansion . . . Jocelyn was right, there had to be a link to the murders. Why else would Harding Scott have had a photo of it? He had been collecting the evidence, had saved it for people like them because he knew he could be in some danger.

Stevie felt in the pit of her knotted stomach that unraveling the corrupt police department was sure to lead her to Gina Walters's and Harding Scott's killers, and she needed the government's help as much as it needed hers.

"I've heard there's some sweet deal between some of the cops and a wealthy guy in town named Bradley Alsop."

Jocelyn straightened, her antennas immediately up,

and set her cheeseburger on the plate. "What kind of deal?"

"I don't know exactly," Stevie replied haltingly, wishing she had more information. "I only just heard this earlier today. But apparently some of the cops hang out regularly with this guy, shoot on his firing ranges, that kind of thing. And he donates to the annual Christmas party."

"Do you know anything about him?" Jocelyn asked.

"Not really, but I'll make some vague inquiries."

Jocelyn nodded idly, preoccupied with her own train of thought. "I'll check him out too."

"I did run his name at work today. He —" Stevie halted abruptly at the darkening of Jocelyn's face. "What?"

There was an edge to Jocelyn's voice as she glanced in alarm at Jovanowski, then back at Stevie. "That wasn't a good idea, Stevie. You should have let us do that." Jocelyn leveled her glare on Stevie and let her have it with both barrels. "Stevie, you've got to be extremely careful, especially since there's no one here to cover your back. If someone in the department regularly checks on CPIC queries, they're going to see that you ran Alsop."

Stevie felt her face crawling, her ego too bruised to allow herself to fear the consequences she couldn't help imagining. "Fuck. I'm sorry." She closed her eyes and mentally slapped herself. Had she relaxed too much, become too cocky in her role, and, as a result, got sloppy? She didn't need to be told that tiny mistakes could be costly in this game of cat and mouse.

Jovanowski sighed almost inaudibly, visibly trying

to dull his distress. "Just make sure you have a believable reason cooked up for querying Alsop if anyone asks."

Jocelyn nodded her agreement, easing off. What was done was done. "All right then, what did you find out?"

Stevie shifted her gaze between them, her voice as deflated as her pride. It reminded her she was still a rookie in this business of murder. "He's forty-six. Has a juvenile record for petty theft, minor assaults, but clean as an adult."

Jocelyn cupped her chin thoughtfully, her dinner momentarily ignored. "So how does a young thug become a self-made millionaire, or whatever he is?"

Stevie and Jovanowski exchanged shrugs, bit into their respective cheeseburgers.

"I'll check out his financial records with Revenue Canada, at least find out what he's legally into," Jocelyn offered.

"By the way," Jovanowski jumped in, his mouth still full. "Nothing on Mercer. I took his prints down to ident, but Kubota's on holiday for a few days."

"Not much on Dales, either," Jocelyn added. "Doesn't appear to be living above his means, though credit card checks show he makes a lot of weekend trips to Niagara."

Stevie looked up quickly from her frothy mug. "Casino? Maybe he's a gambler."

Jocelyn nodded, impressed. "Good thought, Stevie. We can ask around, see if the casino people there recognize his photo. Now if you'll excuse me," she grinned, "this beer doesn't want to stay in this body."

Stevie leaned in closer to her partner, her voice hushed but urgent. "Ted, you know this mansion where Alsop lives? It's the same goddamn place as the one in Harding Scott's photo."

Jovanowski's face paled. "Shit, are you sure?"

Stevie nodded grimly. "Do you think it means what I think it means?"

Jovanowski expelled his full cheeks. "It sure as hell is beginning to sound like Walters, and later Scott, were on to whatever was going on between Alsop and some of these cops."

Stevie nodded, her stomach clenching in response. "And they knocked them off because they were getting too close. That has to be what Dana was talking about when she said Gina was on to something really big." Stevie drummed her fingers on her mug, the rhythm in time with her racing thoughts. "But what about Mercer? Where does he fit into all of this? It could have been just coincidence that he went into a jealous rage at the same time that Gina was finding out about the corruption."

Jovanowski shrugged, out of answers. Both stared glumly into their glasses, sickened by the whole mess unraveling before them. They both knew there was not a damn thing they could do without concrete evidence. And though they should have been sharing this information with Jocelyn, there was an unspoken agreement that they wouldn't alarm Jocelyn. One word from her and the ministry would come in full force, and Stevie and Jovanowski would be out. They weren't ready to bail yet.

Stevie took another swallow of beer and decided not to tell Jovanowski about the patrol cars that had been eerily following her. No need to hit the panic button yet.

* * * * *

Stevie slowed her pace after catching sight of movement behind a tree in front of her apartment building. It was just a flash darting into the shadow of the tree, but she'd seen it. Her eyes scanned the neighborhood for idling cars or figures inside parked cars, but there was nothing, just as no one had appeared to follow her from the bus stop two blocks away.

Stevie sauntered on, casually whistling a Trisha Yearwood song, and it occurred to her that she should have brought more of her country tapes from home. She'd never tell Jade she didn't miss Jade's Motown, jazz, and R & B. She smiled in the cold. Some things were worth putting up with for the sake of marital bliss.

In front of the thick tree now, Stevie suddenly stopped. With catlike quickness, she turned and leaped to the other side just as the shadowy figure did the same. The collision brought an eruption of muffled groans, both bodies tumbling into a heap on the snowy ground.

"Shit, my nose!" the figure squealed.

Stevie extracted herself from the tangle. Her face, her heart, lit up like Times Square on New Year's Eve.

"Jade! What are you doing here?"

Still holding a frozen mitten over her nose, Jade winked, a smile somewhere underneath. "Thought I'd sneak into town and surprise my woman. But I think I was the one who got the surprise."

Stevie helped her up, both brushing snow from their clothes. Stevie's voice dropped to a whisper. "It's dangerous for you to be here. You know that, don't you?"

They hurried to Stevie's building, taking the back stairs, Stevie trying to scold Jade for coming, but smiling the whole time. Jade tried to assuage Stevie's worries, explaining she'd driven to Shelton's train station, parked, then taken a bus to Stevie's. She'd then hid out front, waiting for Stevie.

"I would have gone crazy if another week had gone by without seeing you," Jade implored, once inside Stevie's apartment. "I'm sorry," she said, even though she wasn't.

Stevie grinned, her heart a feather, and hugged Jade with every ounce of her. Ever since she'd come to Shelton, their phone conversations had been somewhat stilted as they ignored the emotional gulf between them. But being together now — it was like nothing had happened.

"God, I missed you, Jade." Stevie squeezed her again. "You don't know how badly I wanted to see you too. Now, let me look at that nose."

It was swelling but didn't look cut or broken. Stevie, playing doctor this time, took a bag of frozen corn from the freezer and held it to Jade's nose while Jade shrugged off her knapsack and coat, and tossed her toque aside.

"Hey, your hair! You cut it short," Stevie said in awe, loving Jade's new short-haired look. Her gaping mouth quickly turned into an approving grin.

Jade smiled. "Another surprise for you."

"I love it! Have you eaten yet?"

Jade nodded, the bag of corn protruding from her face.

"I just came back from dinner with Ted and Jocelyn Travers."

Jade pulled the bag away, grinning wickedly. "I think he's got the major hots for her."

Stevie laughed. "He does, I can tell, and why not? She's good looking, smart, and seems to be single."

Jade rummaged through her knapsack and pulled a bottle of wine from it. Her smile was lusty, her green eyes dark and glinting, full of that smoky, impatient come-fuck-me look Stevie knew and had only dreamed about lately.

Stevie felt herself stirring in response and kissed her lover, quickly apologizing when Jade pulled back, painfully holding her nose again. Stevie took two glasses from the cupboard and opened the bottle with one pull.

"Shall we drink these in the bedroom?" Stevie winked, filling the glasses.

"Thought you'd never ask."

Stevie led her into the small bedroom and set their glasses on the nightstand. Her plans didn't include much time for sipping wine. Maybe afterward . . .

Jade sat on the bed, leaned back on her elbow, stretching out, her jeans lusciously hugging her body like a second and soon-to-be unnecessary skin. "Hey, my little cowgirl. I never have seen you in a uniform. Bet you look *real* good, though." She inhaled deeply, her eyes glowing catlike in the light of the small bedside lamp, her smile a subtle allusion to the fantasy brewing in her mind.

Stevie tilted her head smugly, her wink exaggerated. "I could show you, but it'll cost you."

Jade's eyebrow arched seductively. "What's the price?"

Stevie began pulling her uniform from the closet. "An entire night of sex!"

She could hear Jade laughing as she scurried to the bathroom, carelessly shedding her jeans and sweatshirt in a trail along the way. She returned to the bedroom in her midnight blue wool pants, light blue dress shirt with gold embroidered Shelton Police shoulder flashes, and black clip-on tie. Her forage cap was tilted at a silly angle. She'd have to do without the gun belt, which was in her locker at work.

Jade whistled. "Mmm, you look delicious."

Stevie twirled awkwardly, straightening her hat. "You like?"

Jade's eyes glided admiringly over Stevie's body. "C'mere and I'll show you."

Jade sat up as Stevie knelt in front of her. Jade pulled at the tie then, with her teeth, unclasped it from Stevie's collar and let it drop to the floor, both of them giggling.

"Now, why don't you do the rest?" Jade purred.

Stevie frowned with put-on irritation, then hurriedly began jerking the buttons free.

"No, no," Jade scolded, halting Stevie's hasty hands with her own. "Nice and sl-o-o-o-w. I want to watch."

"Jade, you're being silly."

"C'mon, my little fantasy. Give me something to take back with me."

Relenting, Stevie stood, and, slower this time,

pulled her shirt free and relieved the final two buttons. She stopped long enough to toss her cap onto the bed.

Jade was wound for sound, hooting, whistling, and clapping rhythmically as Stevie playfully tossed the shirt to her. "All of it! Take it all off!"

Jade gasped pleasurably at the sight of Stevie's small firm breasts and muscular shoulders. Too shy to dance, Stevie toyed with the zipper of her pants, triceps bulging.

Jade nodded enthusiastically, hungry for more. She sipped her wine, watched Stevie slowly, tauntingly, slide her pants down her hips. She was totally naked underneath, her body hard, ripe.

No longer able to stand it, Jade jumped up, grabbed Stevie's hand and pulled her to the bed, a laughing Stevie gently collapsing onto her, her pants tangled around her ankles. Jade's lips ravenously attacked Stevie's; instantly she forgot the pain from her swollen nose as Stevie's tongue parted her mouth and explored familiar territory.

"God, I've wanted you so badly," Stevie whispered into the silky, now-short hair, breathing in the sweet shampoo scent. She touched the hair, let it sift through her fingers like fine sand, and vowed, for a reason she couldn't explain, never to forget the feel of it. Nothing was as good as this. *Nothing.*

Gently, she sucked at Jade's neck, nibbling and kissing as her fingers released the buttons of Jade's denim shirt. She felt Jade stir beneath her, a low moan in her throat. Stevie smiled between the kisses, kicked the pants from around her own ankles as she unclasped Jade's bra. She marveled for a moment at the freed, perfectly round breasts, dark nipples taut and inviting.

She felt Jade's hands in her own short, fine hair, tugging urgently as Stevie's mouth embraced a nipple. Jade moaned, louder now, as Stevie's massaging fingers encircled the breasts, her tongue alternately stroking each nipple.

"Oh god, Stevie," Jade murmured breathlessly, her eyes tightly squeezed. "Don't . . . make me . . . wait."

Stevie's left hand slid down and was met with raised hips that pushed up and sank rhythmically as Stevie cupped the pulsating mound, damp even through the jeans. Stevie moved down, unclasping the button of Jade's jeans. Her teeth playfully latched on to the zipper, tugging it slowly, agonizingly down.

"Stevie Houston, you're a brat!"

Stevie looked up, grinning widely.

"God, I love you," Jade laughed, then moaned as her pants were pulled down, damp silk panties parted to one side, Stevie too impatient to slide the underwear right off. Stevie's warm mouth was instantly on her, tongue driving deeply into Jade as Jade pushed back. Stevie's hands cupped her ass and pulled at the same time.

Without warning, her tongue halted its raging mission and lingered over the soft folds of swollen flesh, circling Jade's clitoris, then briskly flicking from side to side.

Jade threw her head back into the pillow, the veins of her neck throbbing, chest heaving with her racing heartbeat. She felt Stevie inside her again. When she came, she impulsively cupped Stevie's head, pulled her into her.

Mouth tightly locked onto her, Stevie rode each wave, feeling Jade's pleasure as if it were rolling through her own body.

Stevie slithered up to her lover and hugged her tightly, not wanting this night to end. But she knew Jade would have to head back home after breakfast, and she would have to get back to being Sarah Houston, Shelton police constable. Not to mention solving this double murder.

"What's the matter, honey?" Jade rolled on top of Stevie. "I felt you stiffen."

Stevie shook her head. "Nothing. Just thinking about this case."

Jade's finger tenderly touched Stevie's lips.

Stevie smiled. "Are you still pissed off at me for being away from you?"

Jade kissed the tip of Stevie's nose. "Honey, you do what you just did to me and I'd forgive anything."

Stevie waggled her eyebrows suggestively. "I'll remember that."

Jade brushed a lock of Stevie's hair from her forehead, looked into the deep brown eyes that were far older than their thirty-one years. "I worry about you, honey. And I miss you terribly. But I know you have a job to do, and I respect what you do. I think you're a great cop, Stevie, and I'm so proud of you."

"You mean that?" Stevie beamed.

"Of course I do. And now I want to show you how much I love you."

Jade kissed her, both never feeling more in love than at this moment. Jade's hand was being guided down to Stevie's already wet apex, Stevie pressing it against her hot flesh, anxious for orgasm and this demonstration of Jade's love.

But Jade was not to be cheated. She wanted to taste Stevie, to revel in her scent, in the plush wetness. And she did, her tongue exploring every slick crevice and protrusion while two of her fingers slipped inside Stevie. She pumped while her tongue moved to its own beat. It wasn't long before the convulsions of orgasm had Stevie quaking and calling out. As Stevie liked to joke, she always found religion when Jade made love to her.

It was well into the early morning hours before their bottle of wine was exhausted and their bodies equally drained from sex, sex that was most often tender but at times raw and boisterous, almost desperate. Both had seen enough in their lifetimes to know that life could often be ugly and fleeting, but that the beauty they found in each other, in their relationship, was real and was to be coveted.

Stevie rolled over and heaved herself from the warm bed, her pleasantly exhausted body feeling thick, like mud. She wanted to brush her teeth, wash up a bit before sleep. She paused at the bedroom window, peeked out between the slats of the blind. Her muscles went rigid as her eyes followed the police car creeping down the street in front of her building.

"What's up?" Jade asked sleepily.

"Nothing, hon. Go to sleep."

CHAPTER ELEVEN

Stevie sipped from the lukewarm paper cup of coffee snug in her gloved hands and shivered in the door stoop. Though still early evening, it was dark. She was cold and aching from having stood outside for the past hour.

Thoughts of Jade and their wonderful evening last night were warming her, though not in the part of her body that needed to be warm at this moment. Jade's surprise visit had excited her, made her happy, but at the same time, reminded her that she'd been in this hellhole for exactly two weeks and there was no sign it'd be over any time soon.

Stevie glanced at her watch. She was supposed to call Jovanowski in ten minutes to see if he and Jocelyn had come up with anything on Bradley Alsop in the last twenty-four hours. She quietly stamped her feet in a futile attempt to ward off the chill gnawing at her.

The outside door of the building across the street opened. Stevie huddled in the shadows, wishing herself invisible.

Kelly Bronskill closed the door behind her just as a sleek black limo pulled up, as if on cue. In the cold, every noise seemed crude and amplified, so when the car's back door opened, then closed for her, it sounded to Stevie like a rifle shot.

Stevie watched the disappearing taillights, committing the plate number to memory. Once it was safely gone, she scanned the empty street, then walked off in search of a phone booth.

"Ted, it's me."

"Hey, Tex," Jovanowksi's sly voice answered her. "Heard you had a visitor last night."

Stevie smiled broadly into the receiver, took a deep, pleasurable breath, exhaled slowly. "Oh, yeah. Did I ever."

Jovanowski chuckled. "I take it you're feeling pretty good today?"

"Definitely," Stevie enthused, marveling at how far Jovanowski had come in three months to be able to joke with her about her sex life. "Though spending a Sunday evening out in the cold isn't exactly my idea of fun. I'd rather do last night all over again."

Jovanowksi laughed, then, full of concern, asked: "Why, what are you up to?"

"I've been keeping my eye on a local hooker. Name's Kelly Bronskill."

"So? C'mon, spill."

"I don't know, Ted. But something's up with her. She's hands off as far as the Shelton Police Department is concerned, because they say she informs for them. But I don't buy it. She's just a two-bit drug user and hooker. And she gets real nervous around me. In fact, everyone gets jumpy if I mention her name."

Jovanowski exhaled loudly. "Just be careful. Somebody may be watching her back for her."

"Funny thing just happened. A big limo came and picked her up." Stevie read off the plate number to him.

"I'll check it out, see who it's registered to. Speaking of checking things out, it seems our boy Alsop deals in computer parts. Ships them in from the U.S., then distributes them here to various buyers."

"Profitable business, I take it?"

"Hugely, by the looks of it. No dirt on him, though he smells like a rat to me. I can't believe computer parts would pay *that* well. You should see his income."

"What about Chief Dales?"

"That was a good guess about the casino. Apparently he does like to gamble there. So he's obviously getting the money from somewhere for his little habit because he doesn't have any huge debts, no second mortgages, that type of thing."

"You want me to try and get closer to Dales or Alsop? I can find out if they're buddies, maybe follow the chief."

"No," Jovanowski barked. "McLemore wants you to stay low for another week or two. Dales or Alsop might get word that someone's checking on them, and they're sure to get *very* paranoid about now."

Stevie sighed her disappointment. "Shit, Ted. I'm getting closer to this thing; I can feel it. I want to wrap it up." God, how she wanted to get home to Jade.

"Stevie, look. Don't blow this, goddammit. You've got to play this cool. It's not just our careers at stake, but your life. So don't do anything stupid. Remember, two cops are already dead."

Stevie exhaled again, knowing she was between the proverbial rock and a hard place. She'd promised McLemore she'd play by the rules this time. *Damn.* "All right. Oh yeah, Mercer's supposed to start on my shift tomorrow morning."

"Good. Maybe you can get a feel for him. But don't do anything obvious. Like I said, play it cool."

"I will, Ted," Stevie promised reluctantly. "I'll be cool. I'm not going to blow this thing, okay?"

He hesitated, as if weighing Stevie's sincerity. "Okay, Tex. And listen. Kubota's back from holiday tomorrow, so I'm going to have him go over Mercer's prints. I want you to call me as soon as you're done your shift tomorrow evening. That should give him plenty of time to analyze those prints. Oh yeah, and call me on your way to work in the morning too. I can tell you about the limo plate."

"OK, Ted. I better go. Take care."

"No, *you* take care, Tex."

Stevie hung up, pulled her coat tightly around her neck, and started for home. It was several blocks and she walked as quickly as her frozen legs would carry her. She was glad no cop cars appeared to be spying on her, and even more glad she hadn't told Jovanowski about that. *He'd have a shit fit.*

The patrol car skulked along the dark street, bright moonlight casting a blue sheen on the fresh snow and on the shiny white car. Headlights extinguished, it came to a halt across from the familiar apartment building. The engine purred; plumes of white exhaust floated skyward.

Stevie jerked awake, images of a gun firing at her still crisp in her mind, the roar still reverberating in her head. It was the second time this same nightmare had haunted her sleep during her stay in Shelton, and, like any time she thought of death, she instinctively thought of her twin sister, Sarah.

She threw the covers from her naked body, shivered in the predawn chill, then scrambled for sweatpants and a T-shirt. She poured herself a shot of bourbon — she still had three hours before reporting to work — and sipped it slowly in the darkness.

Groggy moments later, Stevie padded back toward the bedroom. But something — a nagging feeling of being watched — made her stop at the kitchen window. A shiver traveled up her spine. A police car, its lone occupant shadowed in the darkness, sat parked across the street, engine running, lights off.

Stevie stepped back from the window, rage hammering her gut. Sweat prickled along her hairline and her breath quickened as she decided she wasn't going to take it any more. She sprang to the closet and hastily pulled on boots and jacket. From another

112

boot inside the closet, she plucked out her seven-round semiautomatic Beretta pistol, issued to her specifically for going undercover in Shelton. It was small and light, and she'd made a habit of strapping it to her ankle every time she put on her uniform, just in case she needed a backup gun.

She shoved open the heavy steel fire door, and jogged down the stairs. She'd get the bastard this time, find out who the hell was stalking her.

She crouched at the corner of the building, shoved her hand in her coat pocket, and released the safety on her pistol. She moved quickly, staying low, creeping up to the car on her belly, trying to stay in the car's blind spot and outside the range of mirrors.

Clutching the gun in her pocket with her right hand, she grabbed the passenger door handle with her left, hoping to hell it wasn't locked.

She yanked; the door sprang open. In a flash, Stevie pulled the gun from her pocket, aimed it at the cop in the driver's seat. There was a dual gasp.

"Christ, Sarah! You almost gave me a heart attack." Sue Jackson still had her left hand over her heart, her right hand frozen on her holster.

Stevie's heart was in her throat. She tried to steady her voice, the gun still pointed at her fellow officer. She found her voice, raspy from the adrenaline. "What the hell are you doing spying on me?"

Jackson, her face as washed out as the moonlight, was still gulping for air, nearly hyperventilating. Her hands dropped harmlessly to her sides. "You wanna put that goddamn gun down?"

Stevie lowered it, but didn't thumb the safety back on. "I said, what the fuck game are you playing with me?"

"Look, Sarah. I don't know what you're talking about. I didn't even know you lived here. I was just . . ."

Stevie raised the gun again, her eyes devoid of any emotion, as if this were merely target practice. She was in her cop mode, unwilling to take any shit.

Jackson recoiled at the coldness in Stevie's eyes. "All right! What are you, crazy or something?"

Stevie blinked, her body relaxing a little. "Just tell me what the fuck's going on."

Sue Jackson looked at Stevie, her eyes wide, imploring, frightened still. "I never meant to scare you like this, Sarah. I just . . ." Teardrops slithered down her cheeks, and she swiped at them angrily, her voice quaking. "God, I hate myself like this, Sarah . . . please, don't hate me."

Stevie lowered the gun again, puzzled. "What are you talking about?"

"I want to be with you, Sarah. I want you, OK? I —"

"Aw, Christ," Stevie exhaled in a mixture of relief and newfound anger. She flipped the gun's safety on, shoved it back in her pocket. "You mean that's what this is all about?"

Jackson nodded shyly, then reached across the seat for Stevie's hand.

"Don't fuckin' touch me," Stevie hissed, shaking now as her adrenaline ebbed. "Christ, Sue, you've been scaring me half to death all this time."

Stevie rose from her crouch position and slammed the car door.

Jackson scampered out of the car and stood, elbows resting on the car roof. "Please, Sarah, don't make this ugly."

114

Stevie began stalking back to her building. "It already is ugly. Just stay away from me," she shouted over her shoulder.

Inside the women's locker room, Stevie slipped into her uniform, glad Sue Jackson appeared to have already left from her night shift. She felt a pang of guilt; perhaps she'd been a little hard on her obsessor. Jackson's behavior had been bizarre, for sure, but not worthy of the wrath Stevie had shown her. One day, perhaps Sue Jackson would understand the pressure Stevie was under.

Stevie closed her locker door, then hitched up her leather gun belt. She'd have a talk with Sue when this was all over, make sure she knew Stevie wasn't some homophobic, paranoid bitch given to dramatics.

She joined the others from her shift in the briefing room, listened to a summary of incidents from the night shift, scribbled down names of suspects and plate numbers of stolen cars to be on the lookout for. She avoided eye contact with Kent Mercer on the other side of the conference table, and was surprised when Sergeant Edgar assigned them to partner up for the shift.

Stevie found it hard to make small talk with the man, whose body language exuded negativity and aloofness. The giant chip on his shoulder was too much for her to try to dislodge, so they rode mostly in silence, Stevie thinking about Kelly Bronskill and the limo. Jovanowski had told her the plate was registered to a numbered company owned by Bradley Alsop. Stevie was anxious to talk to the little waif again, find out what the hell she was doing with Alsop. Finally, she was beginning to link evidence in this case. She envisioned a triangle in her mind, with the Shelton police on one end, Bradley Alsop on the other, and Bronskill at the tip. Right now, she was the only concrete link between the two.

"Car 3," the dispatcher broke in over the car's two-way radio.

Mercer picked up the handheld microphone. "Car 3, go ahead."

"Attend a domestic disturbance at 1440 Sullivan Avenue."

"Ten-four. Any particulars, dispatch?"

"Neighbors called it in. They say they can hear loud arguing between two women inside."

"Ten-four." Mercer shoved the mike back in its metal holder and made a left at the next intersection. He glanced at Stevie and made a face. "Sounds like a little lovers' spat to me."

Stevie ignored the comment. She already knew what a homophobic asshole he was, and she wasn't going to pretend she was one as well.

They could hear the yelling and shrieking from the driveway as they pulled in and quickly scurried to the door. It wasn't locked.

Stevie grabbed the first woman, about Jade's size, while Mercer pulled the bigger one aside.

"What's going on here?" Stevie demanded of the two disheveled, red-faced women, who Stevie guessed were both in their early forties, and definitely dykes.

The big one, nearly Stevie's height but on the plump side, began crying softly. Her hands trembled as she rubbed downcast eyes, her voice wavering. "She hit me, Officer."

"C'mon, get serious," Mercer snorted, hitching up his pants. He was a cop who'd seen it all before and this one wasn't about to pull anything on *him*. "She's half your size. How many times did *you* hit her, huh?"

Jerk, Stevie muttered under her breath. "Are either of you injured?" Stevie asked them, looking from one to the other. Though she saw no visible signs of injuries, it was her duty to ask. "Do either of you need medical attention?"

They both shook their heads before the bigger of the two stalked off to the kitchen. The smaller woman crossed her arms over her chest and leaned against the wall.

"There's nothing going on here, Officer. Just a little argument, that's all."

Stevie studied the woman's eyes, saw the confidence melt, a crack in her defiance. She couldn't hold Stevie's stare, and instantly Stevie knew this woman had indeed been the aggressor.

Stevie stepped up to her. "Listen to me. You need help if you're hitting your girlfriend."

She stared at the floor. "I don't need no help."

"Yes, you do," Stevie persisted, ignoring Mercer's relentless fidgeting. "You're going to ruin your relationship, if you haven't already. If your girlfriend's smart, she'll boot you out until you get some counseling and prove that you're better."

The woman's bottom lip began trembling. "She's fucking around on me, I swear," she whispered hoarsely. "I can't put up with that."

Stevie was only inches from her now, her forefinger in the woman's chest. "It doesn't matter. You don't hit someone, not for any reason. Do you want to end up in jail?"

Stevie left her to ponder such a bleak future and went to the victim.

"You okay?" she asked her.

The woman nodded slowly.

"She hurt you?"

A shake of the head.

"Has she done this before?"

A hesitant nod.

"Look," Stevie said, her voice softening. "You don't have to put up with this." She fished a card from her wallet and gave it to the woman. She collected the cards of shelters, psychologists, and social workers for just this purpose. "This is the number for the women's shelter in town. They'll put you up for as long as you need. Do you want us to proceed with charges?"

The woman wiped a tear from her cheek, shook her head. "It'll work out. She just gets paranoid sometimes. She thinks I'm having an affair with my best friend. I *have* been spending a lot of time with my friend lately. It's understandable, I guess. But I'll cool it with my friend for a while, then Leanne'll be just fine."

Stevie had heard all the rationalizations a million times before. She sighed in annoyance. They could still charge the aggressor, but without any visible injuries, no independent witnesses, and an uncooperative victim, the charges wouldn't even make it to court.

Mercer hovered in the kitchen doorway. "You about finished in here, Houston?"

Stevie ignored him. "Listen, this pattern of violence is just going to continue, no matter what you do to alter your behavior. Your girlfriend needs some help; you both do. And if you can't find it here in Shelton, then make the two-hour trip to Toronto and go to 519 Church Street. It's the gay and lesbian community center, and they can tell you where to go for help, all right?"

The woman hesitated before nodding warily.

Stevie and Mercer climbed back into the cruiser, Mercer slamming his door and grunting irritably.

"Christ, why'd you bother playing psychologist with those two queers in there?"

Stevie stared straight ahead as they backed out of the driveway, her voice even. "Because if they don't get help, we could end up back here investigating a murder."

"C'mon, that bigger one can defend herself. Hell, she could clean that little one's clock if she wanted."

Stevie shook her head in exasperation. This guy just wasn't going to get it. She hadn't come across domestic violence in the gay community very often, but she knew it happened, just as it did in heterosexual homes. It was all too easy to assume that women didn't hit each other, except sometimes they did.

Stevie couldn't imagine Jade hitting her, or herself hitting Jade. She had never hit a friend or a lover, but could she? She glanced at her hands, which were strong, nimble. She *did* have a temper. Could anyone be provoked to hit their lover? What if she caught Jade in bed with someone, would that be enough to push her over the edge? She was disturbed by the thought, and even more so by the unknown.

She found herself wondering what Mercer had done when he found out his wife Jan was having an affair with Gina Walters. Had he taken it all out on Gina in some murderous rage? Had he made Jan pay on a daily basis?

Mercer was rambling, Stevie too lost in her thoughts to have heard him.

"What?" she asked distractedly.

"I said, how the hell do you know about this Church Street place in Toronto?"

Stevie looked at him, her eyes scornful. "I just know, okay?"

"What are you, queer too?" he sneered.

"Give it a rest, Mercer. Your attitude is about thirty years out of date."

"Ahh, what the fuck do you know anyway," he smoldered, his eyes fixed on the road ahead.

Stevie turned toward Mercer as he eased the car down a quiet side street.

"Mercer, I know about your wife and Gina Walters." Stevie tried the sympathetic route, but she knew she wasn't doing a very good job of sounding convincing. Still, if she could just push him a little, see what he was made of . . . "I heard the locker-room talk."

He wouldn't look at her, stared blankly at the horizon instead. He swallowed hard, his voice shrinking. "It's none of your damn business."

Stevie opened her mouth, ready to jab the needle in another inch. But the trembling in his hands stopped her. She closed her mouth, surprised at his still-raw pain.

* * * * *

Stevie shared Jovanowski's disappointment. Kubota had tacked an extra day onto his holiday. He wouldn't be back until tomorrow morning to compare Mercer's prints with those taken from Gina and Dana's home after the break-in.

Stevie sat back in her chair and muted the volume on the television. She sipped her drink. If she could shake Mercer for a while tomorrow, she'd go search for Bronskill, have a talk with her. She'd do it tonight if she weren't so damned tired. Bronskill could wait another day. After all, McLemore and Jovanowski wanted her to take it slow.

Stevie took another long swallow. It didn't feel slow at all. On the contrary, she felt like things were rushing toward her, felt like she was being sucked into a vortex.

CHAPTER TWELVE

Jovanowski nervously wiped his forehead with his handkerchief as Kubota furiously typed commands into his computer. The detective had known by Kubota's uncharacteristic excitement on the phone that he'd found something, probably a match on the prints from Dana Jeffries's house.

A split screen appeared on the monitor, with four fingerprints on each side. Both sets looked identical.

Kubota pointed at the prints on the left. "These are Constable Kent Mercer's prints, taken from his personnel files your partner was able to retrieve. Both thumbs and the middle and index fingers of the right hand."

Jovanowski nodded at the obvious. He was used to these scientific types, knew you had to let them go about things at their own pace.

"And over here," the technician pointed to the right side of the screen, "are the prints you gave me that were lifted from a home in Shelton by Detective Harding Scott."

Jovanowski nodded again, wiping his forehead for the umpteenth time. God, what he wouldn't do for a cigarette about now. "And they're a match, right?"

"Right," Kubota smiled.

Jovanowski straightened, relieved at the proof Mercer had indeed broken into Jeffries's house, probably in an attempt to get the diary and destroy any other evidence of Walters's affair with his wife, trying to cover his tracks so there was no evidence he had a motive in killing Walters. Or maybe he was planning to murder Scott by the time he broke in —

"That's not all," the small Oriental man interrupted Jovanowski's thoughts. "I also spent the morning going through the case file you left me. I know you didn't request it, but I looked at the prints collected from the car in which Detective Scott's body was found."

Jovanowski's thick, gray eyebrows abruptly sliced into his heavily lined forehead. "And?"

Kubota shook his head. "First thing I noticed is they're exactly from the same fingers as the prints from the house: two thumbs and the middle and index fingers of the right hand. Strange . . ."

Jovanowski rubbed his eyes irritably, reminding himself to be patient.

123

Kubota tapped a few more keys. "You see on the right here? These are the prints from the car."

Jovanowski peered at the screen. Holy shit, he breathed, his heart thumping faster. "They match!"

Kubota smiled and pointed to the corresponding markers in the sets of prints; plenty of them proved they were an exact match.

Jovanowski leaped up from his chair; he had to reach Stevie. A hand lightly pulled him back.

"Wait, Detective Jovanowski, that's not all."

Jovanowski sat heavily, a sense of gloom settling in his stomach just as heavily as a Big Mac. He had the distinct feeling he wasn't going to like what he was about to hear.

Kubota tapped another key. Mercer's prints were instantly enlarged so that the fingerprints looked more like a black and white crayon sketch from a child.

With the eraser nub of his pencil, Kubota pointed to a couple of tiny, opaque dots on the prints. "See these little pinprick-size dots here? It was driving me crazy. I couldn't figure out what they were at first. In fact I noticed them on the prints you gave me that came from that house, and now these same dots in exactly the same place on the prints from the car."

"So, what are you saying?"

Kubota scratched his head. "At first I thought these dots were some weird aberration in the way they were lifted, or contaminants on the skin or the surface from which the prints were taken. But I ask myself: Why would they appear identical on both sets, which were lifted by different police departments and months apart? And why just these same four fingers from both crime scenes?" He shook his head. "They're all so perfect too — no smudges or anything."

Jovanowski was lost, quickly growing disinterested in Kubota's hypothesizing. "Look, I appreciate what you've put into this case, Kubota. But I really need to get this information to my partner."

Kubota smiled charitably. "I know that, Detective. But do you know what those little dots are?"

Jovanowski sighed, shook his head, and played the part of the dumb student.

"They're air bubbles," Kubota smiled triumphantly, like he'd just single-handedly discovered a new galaxy.

Jovanowski looked baffled. "Air bubbles? What the hell is that supposed to mean?"

Kubota called up the prints lifted from Jeffries's house and Scott's car, and then expanded them until they were unrecognizable. "I've only seen this once before, and it was during an experiment at a forensic training seminar."

Kubota pointed at the screen to a corresponding spot on the edge of the fingerprint samples. "See this little line here? It appears exactly the same in each print from both crime scenes."

"Yeah, so what does it mean?"

Kubota's smile was one of barely contained enthusiasm. "It's the edge of a molded rubber stamp."

"Huh?" Jovanowski was lost.

"These prints were faked, Detective. I've never actually seen it in a real case before. But several of us tried it once as an experiment to see if it could be done."

Jovanowski couldn't decide whether he was

shocked or just plain pissed off. Everything about this case seemed to lead down a new path, with nothing but stone walls at every turn. "You're sure about this?" he asked halfheartedly, knowing already what the answer was.

"Of course I'm sure. It's the only thing that makes sense."

"So you're saying someone made a rubber mold of Mercer's prints from his hands?"

"Exactly. See, you take a soft pliable substance, like putty or plasticine, and place it to the person's fingers. Then, with a good mold substance, like dental rubber, you make a cast from it. And there you have it. You can leave all the prints you want. Sounds simple, but it's not quite that easy, and that's why there were these air bubbles — the cast wasn't perfect." Kubota looked at the screen admiringly. "Though I must say they did a pretty good job."

Jovanowski ran a hand over his neglected stubble, silently wondering how the conspirators took imprints from Mercer's fingers. If he were drunk and passed out, or asleep, he supposed it was possible. It had been years since Jovanowski worked patrol, but he remembered how tired a cop could get on those endless night shifts, and it wasn't unusual for partners to take turns sleeping in the car if everything was quiet.

He stood up and made for the door, more slowly this time. "Listen, I owe you one, Kubota."

Stevie was as surprised by the development as Jovanowski had been, and both were stumped by what it meant. Why would someone want to set Mercer up to make it look like he'd broken into Dana Jeffries's house as well as murdered Harding Scott?

"It had to be someone in the department," Stevie mused over the phone to Jovanowski. "Otherwise the Shelton investigators would have lifted the prints at Dana's after the break-in, instead of Harding Scott coming up with them a day or so later. The department either missed the prints altogether or planted them."

"And don't forget Dana Jeffries could have been in on it."

Stevie's face soured into a doubtful frown. "Either way, someone wanted Harding Scott to find Mercer's prints in that house after the break-in. Why though? To make it look like he'd killed Gina and was covering his tracks?"

There was a pause before Jovanowski spoke. "Could be, if this person knew Harding Scott had already discovered Gina's supposed suicide was actually a murder. Then they killed Scott and left Mercer's prints behind to make it look like Mercer was protecting himself from Scott implicating him in Gina's murder."

Stevie exhaled heavily into the receiver. "Unfortunately, your little scenario makes sense. So someone wants us to arrest Mercer for Harding Scott's murder." Stevie was silent for a moment as she gathered her thoughts. "Someone wanted Walters, Scott and Mercer out of the way — two of them murdered and one implicated in the murders. Mercer must know something pretty explosive."

"I'm assuming Mercer doesn't know his prints are all over those two crime scenes," Jovanowski jumped in. "We need to come clean with him, take him under our protection and find out who he thinks wanted to set him up. But we need him on our side first."

"He called in sick today," Stevie said, wincing to herself at the memory of the uncomfortable scene in the locker room earlier that morning. Sue Jackson had been called to fill in for Mercer on the shift, and she hadn't been able to look Stevie in the eye. Both spoke only the minimal words necessary between coworkers.

"Maybe you should run by and check on him," Jovanowski suggested, his tone indicating worry.

"You think his life is in imminent danger?"

"Who the hell knows. But the closer we get, the more this thing feels like a powder keg."

Stevie hung up and hopped back into her patrol car. She threaded the car through the early afternoon traffic to Kent Mercer's address, purposely not radioing in her location. She had half an eye out for Kelly Bronskill on the way. She still needed to find the young prostitute and put the screws to her. Time to press her in no uncertain terms as to what her connection to Bradley Alsop was.

Kent Mercer, looking like hell, finally opened the door after a couple of minutes of persistent knocking. His T-shirt was discolored with yesterday's coffee stains, his face puffy and unshaven, his hair disheveled, his feet bare. His hand loosely gripped half a mickey of Jack Daniel's.

"What the fuck do you want?" he groaned.

Stevie frowned, undeterred. "Can I come in for a minute?"

After a long, bloodshot glare, he clumsily stood aside to allow her in. "Do whatever the fuck you want," he slurred dyspeptically, liquor heavy on his breath.

The condition of the inside of the house looked as fractious and slovenly as Mercer himself. Stevie could see dirty dishes piled incongruously on the kitchen counter, discarded clothing and empty beer cans littering the unvacuumed floor.

"You all right?" Stevie asked tenuously, wondering what had set Mercer into this tailspin. Something obviously had. "I was worried when you called in sick; thought you might need something."

"Yeah, right," he spat before taking another sloppy swig from his bottle as they stood awkwardly in the front hall. "Whaddaya really want, Houston?"

Stevie followed the faint drone of the television to the living room and, brushing crumbs from the sofa seat, sat down uninvited. Mercer resentfully followed and finally slumped in a stained wingback chair.

"Where's your wife?" Stevie asked not so innocently, steering the conversation into his personal life.

Mercer shrugged complacently, swallowing another mouthful. "Gone."

"You mean gone, as in left?"

Mercer didn't answer. He stared vacantly at the images on the television screen, his eyes liquor glazed.

Stevie intertwined her thumbs, twirled them, unsure of how far she should go with Mercer. She had to wait for Jovanowski before they confronted him with everything they knew. Yet, on an obvious emotional precipice, Mercer was ripe for the plucking now, and she waded in.

"This isn't just about your wife leaving you, is it?"

Stevie said in a knowing whisper, spreading her arms to include him, the room. "You're in trouble, Mercer."

His eyes slowly shifted to hers, and though they wouldn't focus, there was a skittish desperation in them. She knew his apathy was a poorly attempted ruse to throw her off, or maybe even to deceive himself.

Leaning on the edge of her seat now, Stevie sucked in her breath before she spoke. "Like I told you yesterday, I know about your wife and Gina Walters." Her voice was low, her eyes earnest. "It must have just about killed you, knowing your wife was getting it from another woman."

Mercer's face reddened, his fists clenched in anger. Then he shrugged, feigning sudden indifference, wiped his nose with the back of his hand. "That was years ago. It was no big deal. We got over it."

Stevie loosely locked her fingers together, still leaning forward, her voice calmly challenging. "C'mon, I know cops are competitive. No cop wants to lose his woman to another cop. And the guys at work must have made your life hell over it."

Mercer stared at the floor, melting into a slump.

"Hell, Walters was a *detective,* not just a patrol officer like you." Stevie sat back, satisfied with the fresh bait she had just offered, but casting a bit more. She shook her head in empathy. "And a woman too. Shit, Mercer. Losing your wife to a woman, and a woman who was higher ranked than you must have —"

"Motherfuckers just didn't know what it was like," Mercer said, barely audible. "They just couldn't fuckin' let it rest." His voice picked up like an approaching locomotive. "Every day, every goddamn day, they just

130

couldn't let me forget it." He caught himself about to become a runaway mess and tried to shunt his wanton emotions. He clammed up.

Stevie waited calmly, let him gather himself again. "Why did you take it out on Gina? Why did you leave her threatening notes?"

Mercer hugged his bottle protectively between his legs, shrugged, his voice growing contrite. "I just wanted her to know she couldn't get away with it so easily. I thought she deserved to feel some of what I was feeling."

Stevie exhaled in frustration. What a sad excuse of a man, she opined to herself. She leaned forward again, wanting to gauge every inch of his reaction to her next comment. "Gina Walters died shortly after. There's talk it wasn't suicide — that it was murder. Haven't you been worried all this time that you might be fingered for her murder? After all, her stealing your wife is a pretty good motive."

Mercer's hands began to tremble, and he stared uncertainly at Stevie for a long time, his reddened eyes straining for clarity as if really seeing Stevie for the first time. "Who the fuck are you?" he asked thinly, his question not accusatory or condemning, but rather full of urgent curiosity.

Stevie stood, adjusted her thick leather gun belt and its dangling leather and steel accoutrements. "It doesn't matter who I am. But if you're worried about anything, Mercer, anything at all, or if you just want to talk, you can come to me." She made her way to the door, whispered over her shoulder. "I'm not one of *them*."

Stevie drove slowly through the streets of Shelton, chewing about her visit with Kent Mercer. Had she said too much? Pushed him too far? She knew she wasn't the only one putting the screws to him, judging by his current state. His boat was being rocked by someone else, and sooner or later it was going to tip if he didn't reach out for help to steady his life.

It was mid-afternoon now, Stevie realized, her growling stomach reminding her she hadn't eaten lunch yet. She wheeled the patrol car down a narrow side street on a shortcut to a deli that made the best pastrami sandwiches this side of heaven.

She braked to a screeching halt. Kelly Bronskill sat, as still as a statue on the curb, her knees drawn up under her winter parka, her chin poised on the palm of her bare hand.

Stevie jumped out of the car, leaving the door wide open, and squatted in front of the young woman. Stevie tilted her face up, saw the vacant eyes, mismatched pupils. *Shit. Strung out.*

"Kelly," she shouted, trying to get through the gauze of whatever kind of high Bronskill was on. "I need to talk to you. C'mon, I'll get you a cup of coffee, something to eat."

Stevie pulled her up, and to her surprise, was met with only silence and passive compliance.

CHAPTER THIRTEEN

Kelly Bronskill took the hamburger Stevie bought her from the McDonald's drive-thru and ate it ravenously while Stevie, longing for her pastrami sandwich, nibbled on her fries. The patrol car idled in the parking lot of an abandoned warehouse on the edge of town.

After they'd crumpled their wrappings into the empty bag, Stevie worked on gaining the young hooker's trust. Just maybe she could get enough information out of her to pin that slimy Alsop.

She could look out for her, Stevie promised. She

knew how vulnerable someone like Kelly was, and told her how there would always be someone wanting to own her, calling in favors, letting her do all the dirty work while they greased their own palms from a comfortable distance.

But Stevie's attempts bounced off the unresponsive Bronskill, who fumbled silently in her worn purse for a cigarette. Her quivering hands put one to her mouth.

Stevie punched the lighter in the dash, held the glowing knob to the cigarette.

Frustrated, Stevie resorted to Plan B. "Look Kelly, I know you're into something way over your head. I know you're involved with Alsop and some of the cops in this city. You wanna tell me about it, or do I have to find out the hard way?"

Bronskill's insolent eyes tried to hold Stevie's gaze but soon faltered as she spoke in even tones. "I don't know what the hell you're talkin' about, lady."

"Oh, I think you do," Stevie said, her voice flat. She gripped Bronskill's forearm to drive home her point. "I'm going to find out, you know. And you'll be right in the middle of all this mess. Your ass will be in jail for a long time, do you know that?"

Bronskill tried to free her scrawny arm, but couldn't from Stevie's viselike grip.

"And I'm not talking about the county jail, Kelly. I'm talking pen time, and I'm talking years. And you know what?" Stevie hissed. "The other prisoners'll hate you, because word'll get to them that you're a police informant. They'll fuck you up, Kelly. And you won't even be able to hide behind your booze and heroin, because you won't get any in prison."

134

Bronskill smirked her disbelief.

Stevie leaned closer, the muscles of her clenched jaw sinewy, like rope. "I'm not kidding around here, Kelly. You think your buddies on the department will protect you? You think they'll keep me from charging you, is that it?"

Bronskill started to smile then, until the realization that just maybe this cop wasn't bluffing began to sink in. Her shrug was indolent, as if to say she didn't care what this know-it-all told her.

Stevie leaned back, relaxing into haughtiness. "You're making a big mistake by not talking to me, Kelly. Alsop and every dirty cop in this department are going down, and you're going down with them."

A glimmer of panic rose in the hooker's green eyes, which frantically began to search for some invisible escape from all her problems. She puffed the cigarette furiously.

"I know about them, Kelly. And once the shit starts to fly, they're all going to run for cover like rats on a sinking ship. They're not gonna give a shit about you. But I do. I can help you, Kelly, if you'll help me first."

"How do I know this isn't some trick?" her voice crackled like a distant radio.

Stevie rolled her eyes. "Look, why would I want to fuck you around?" Stevie knew that some cops did like to play head games with people like Kelly, just for the power of it, but not her. "Look, Kelly, this thing is bigger than me or you. How long have you been working the streets here?"

Bronskill shrugged, wary, still not believing this wasn't some kind of nasty little trap. "A few years."

"Do you remember a woman cop here from a few years back? She was a street cop, then became a detective. Gina Walters."

Bronskill nodded slightly.

"She died, Kelly. They said it was suicide, but it wasn't. She was murdered, Kelly. And do you know why?"

A tepid shake of the head.

Stevie leaned close again, her eyes afire. She was outraged all over again that cops would kill other cops for their own greed. Cops had enough enemies out there without killing one another. "She was murdered because she was on the verge of finding out about Alsop and his gang of cops."

The quavering moved from Bronskill's hands to her bottom lip as she sat, wide-eyed and slack jawed, watching Stevie.

"And she wasn't the only one. Another Shelton cop, Harding Scott, was murdered last year for the same reason." Stevie let her words echo in the car, waited for their severity to take root in the woman beside her. She whispered, "You want that to happen to you, Kelly? You already know too much, you know. And they'll know you've been talking to me. You see, it won't take them long to realize I'm on to them, and since you've been seen with me, well . . ."

Bronskill jabbed in the direction of the door handle, violently clawing for it, but Stevie had already locked all the doors, and only the push of her power button could open them.

"Let me out!" the woman shrieked, trying for the window now, which wouldn't budge.

136

"Calm down, Kelly," Stevie uttered quietly, waiting for the tantrum to pass.

"They won't kill me, they won't!" Bronskill sobbed. "I don't believe you, you — you bitch!"

"They will, Kelly, they'll take you out. And it'd be damn easy. All they'd have to do is scoop you up, hold you down, and overdose you with a needle full of heroin. Everyone knows you're a junkie, and the coroner will just think it was accidental."

Bronskill's twiglike hands shrouded her face, the stub of her cigarette dropping to the floor.

"There's only one way out of all this, and I think you know what that is," Stevie offered, like a wise parent. "I'm all you have left, Kelly."

Stevie shifted the car into gear and drove off, heading out of town. She radioed in that she would be ten-seven, without giving an explanation to dispatch.

"Tell me all about it, Kelly."

Stevie felt surprisingly calm, almost detached, as Kelly Bronskill confided everything she knew. She told how, six years ago as a sixteen-year-old high school dropout, she'd first been introduced to Bradley Alsop. He liked teenaged girls, was screwing a couple of others at the same time as her, she said. Naive and attracted to the older man and his money, Bronskill thought she was in love with him. But he left her cold. Told her that, at eighteen, she was getting too old for him. But she still wanted to be part of his life any way she could, so she partied regularly at his mansion and did whatever he wanted her to.

"What kind of parties?" Stevie asked. "Drugs, or what?"

Bronskill nodded. "Coke, heroin, anything you wanted. That's how I got into all this. There was sex too — group sex, one-on-one, anything and everything."

"Did Alsop pay you for it? Is that how you got into hooking?"

Another nod. "I didn't mind the sex at first, but after a few months, it wasn't fun anymore — these guys getting all tanked up, then wanting to stick it to you. Some of them would get pretty rough, too. So Bradley started paying me."

Her detachment suddenly gone, Stevie fumed, grinding her molars. *Bastard*. Turning a young girl into a junkie and a hooker. Deserves to have his nuts lopped off. "Were cops at these parties?"

Bronskill hesitated, nodded as she bit her lip.

"Who? Give me names, Kelly."

She uttered a handful of names. Stevie was only mildly surprised at Chief Bob Dales's name.

"Dales only came to a few of these parties at first, and then he stopped. Some of the others only came out a few times too, but it didn't matter."

"What do you mean?" Stevie asked tersely.

"Bradley had hidden video cameras all over, through mirrored glass and stuff. He has everything on tape — the drugs, the orgies."

Stevie clamped her mouth shut. So that's how Alsop got these cops in his pocket. Show them a good time and get it all on tape for blackmailing. With that kind of evidence, they'd do time, and no cop wants to end up in jail with the people he's put in there. So they acted as Alsop's pawns.

"I take it these guys knew they were on tape?"

Bronskill laughed. "They didn't like it at first, that's why some of them never came back. Others,

138

though, they figured what the hell, and it became a joke after a while."

Stevie felt sick to her stomach. "Who else goes to these parties?"

"I don't know their names, but I heard a few of them are customs officers."

Great, Stevie thought bitterly. Not only had Alsop corrupted the local police force, but Canada Customs officials as well. Which meant he must be involved in shipping or receiving something illegal across the border.

Stevie pulled the car into the parking lot of a rundown motel complex. "Have you left anything out, Kelly? Can you tell me what kind of business your friend Bradley is in?"

Bronskill shook her head. "One time, when I asked too many questions, one of his goons slapped me up pretty good."

Stevie noticed the deeply engraved sadness in the premature lines around her eyes, her mouth — lines distinct even in the dusky light.

"I don't ask anymore."

"You made the right decision today, Kelly. I'm going to put you up in this motel until tomorrow, then I'll be back, along with some other out-of-town police officials. I don't want you talking to anyone, understand?"

Bronskill nodded, her streetwise, sassy demeanor having relented to fear and dependency.

"Don't answer the door, the phone, nothing. When I come for you tomorrow, I'll call you the name we're going to register you by. Let's say, Chantel Hewitson."

A smile percolated on the young woman's face, lending her an instant and all too rare youthfulness, and Stevie was suddenly reminded that cops, including herself, sometimes too quickly judged people like Kelly as nothing better than trash. She felt ashamed of her past disdain.

"I like the name Chantel. It's so beautiful," the young woman beamed.

Stevie sped back toward town, far surpassing the speed limit. She needed to call Jovanowski right away and tell him about the latest development with Kelly Bronskill. She needed him here; things were breaking quickly now. But she wanted to drive past Kent Mercer's first. All day she'd been feeling unsettled about him, about his state. And right now, he was a large piece of this puzzle. She hoped, prayed, he'd just drunk himself to sleep.

It was March 3, but dusk still came early. The gray afternoon was fusing to a charcoal evening when the urgent and breathless voice of the dispatcher broke over the radio.

"All units. Attend 120 Johns Avenue for an attempted suicide. Gunshot wound. Ambulance has been called."

Stevie felt the air sucked from her lungs as she stepped on the accelerator. It was Kent Mercer's house.

"Car 5 to dispatch," Stevie shouted into the mike. "I'm almost there."

Stevie's patrol car cut across the lawn, and she jumped out, door gaping open, and leaped up onto the porch with one graceful step. She ran into the house, where a shellshocked, dark haired woman leaned over a prone body on the living room floor.

Stevie touched the woman's shoulder and pulled her back. Kent Mercer lay on his back in his under= wear, his head resting in a pool of blood, his eyelids fluttering in a battle for consciousness.

"Kent, it's me, Sarah," Stevie yelled at him, her head bent close. His right ear was missing; blood poured out from the side of his head. A revolver lay on the floor beside him, and Stevie tried not to inhale too deeply the metallic odor of blood and the acrid dust of gunpowder.

"I just came by to get some things," the woman sobbed. "I heard the gun go off as I came up the driveway —"

"Are you Jan?" Stevie guessed.

The woman nodded through her tears.

"Jan, go get a towel, now! We have to stop the blood flow." She turned her attention back to Mercer as his wife left the room. "Kent, listen to me. You've got to stay conscious. Stay with me now, do you understand? Everything's going to be all right."

Stevie's stomach was still back in the car somewhere, and by no means did she feel everything was going to be fine. But she did her best to stay calm, in control. She held the towel Jan gave her up to Mercer's head and pressed firmly, trying at the same time to wipe away the disconcerting thought that this was all somehow her fault.

* * * * *

141

Bradley Alsop flicked a stray lock of graying hair from his forehead, then meticulously straightened his ponytail. He smiled confidently at his reflection in the oval mirror, his shoulders and chest instinctively stiffening.

Hell, what wasn't there to smile about. Still had his looks, all the money he could want, cars, women . . . Life was pretty damn good for this forty-six-year-old son of a fisherman who'd worked his way up from a shipping and receiving clerk on the docks of Lake Ontario.

The sound of an approaching truck's grinding gears caught his attention and he glanced at his watch. The weekly shipment was on time — clockwork, as usual. Not much went wrong in Bradley Alsop's daily routine. But then, he was a man well prepared, plotting out every last detail. His life was like a Swiss watch, and he was the master tradesman.

The leather chair softly hissed as he sat down and flipped open the black walnut cigar box on his desk. He selected a Cuban Cohiba, rolled it pleasurably between his fingers, under his nose. He clipped the end off with a pair of gold-plated scissors and lit it, smiling as he inhaled, smug because, just a few miles away across the border, Cuban cigars couldn't be bought on the open market. But here, in Canada, it was one of his pleasures he could buy legally. He offered them freely to the Americans he did business with, liked to rub it in.

"Bradley?" It was *never* Brad. The door of his home office tentatively clicked open.

Alsop exhaled a cloud of smoke, squinted through it. "What is it, Jack?"

The look on Jack Mancuso's face told him immediately it was bad news. Surly on the best of days, Mancuso looked downright ugly as he entered the thickly carpeted room. His naturally dark, Mediterranean skin was a deep shade of red, his mouth cemented in a scowl.

"It's Kelly Bronskill," he growled, hands stiffly clasped behind his broad back. "We went to pick her up a few minutes ago for the party tonight, and she wasn't at her usual place."

Alsop frowned. He'd nearly forgotten it was Tuesday — the weekly night of fun and games he threw for the boys. He usually made himself scarce by the time the parties began, letting his cameras and his trusty assistants make sure everyone was having a good time.

He waved his cigar irritably. "All right, so get one of the others. And when Bronskill does show up again, give her a little reminder that it's not nice to miss her weekly appointment."

"I don't think she's coming back," Mancuso growled.

Alsop shrugged. What the hell, she was used up and burned out anyway these days. Probably time to upgrade to something more than a third-string hooker. "All right, then. Cut her loose. You know the procedure."

Mancuso fidgeted, sighing heavily and shoving his beefy hands into his pants pockets. "We can't find her anywhere. And the word from one of our snitches is she was last seen with a cop."

Alsop's senses ripened, his ears prickling. "What cop? One of the boys?"

Mancuso grimly shook his head. "A woman cop. Name of Houston. Hired a couple of weeks ago, apparently."

Alsop set his cigar in the chunky crystal ashtray, rubbed his chin roughly. Dales hadn't told him about this new one. "Any idea what that's about?"

"They took off together in a cop car a couple of hours ago. Apparently this Houston has been seen with her once before." He hedged, shifted his feet.

"What?" Alsop demanded irritably.

"I heard this broad's been asking questions around town about you and I think it was her who drove by here real slow last week."

"Fuck," Alsop swore. He didn't need this shit. Why the hell wasn't Dales doing his damn job? And why hadn't he been told earlier about all of this?

"You want me to take care of her, too?" Mancuso cracked his knuckles.

Alsop firmly shook his head. "Not yet, not until I say." He snatched up his cigar, clamped it between his teeth. "Better cancel tonight. Might have other things to keep us busy. And I want the screws tightened on Mercer, in case Wonder Woman has got to him."

Mancuso's lips twitched in a wisp of a smile. "Already taken care of. He's been told his options, boss."

Mancuso closed the door behind him, Alsop staring hard at it, his gray eyes pinched, unblinking. He shook his head lightly. Another self-righteous, self-inflated cop out to save the world. Oh well, she wasn't the first . . .

Bradley Alsop reached for the phone.

* * * * *

144

Chief Bob Dales scrolled through the computer messages, tapped a couple more keys. His eyes, weary from a ten-hour day, fixed blearily on the screen.

He'd check the past week's CPIC inquiries before going home. He liked to see whose names his officers ran through the national police computer system. It was a way for him to keep tabs on the local criminals, or potential criminals, and it was a good test of which officers were out there doing their jobs and which ones were hiding in the coffee shops.

His eyes roamed down the monitor until they widened in heart-pounding alarm at the sight of Bradley Alsop's name. He checked the time and date, the code number of the officer who'd run Alsop's name. Read it twice, three times. Dales's hand came to his forehead, rested uncertainly there. Sarah Houston was the cop.

The phone rang, startling him while his thoughts were still trying to gel.

Bradley Alsop ranted, Dales having to hold the phone out from his ear to ease the shouting. Did he know this cop Sarah Houston had been checking up on him? Did he, Dales, know Kelly Bronskill had just hours ago been spirited off by Houston? Who the hell was this broad anyway, and why hadn't Dales kept closer tabs on her?

Dales felt his hand quiver, winced as his stomach knotted up. He listened to Alsop, who was less frenzied with each second, and knew, even before it was spelled out, that it would have to happen all over again. Another Shelton cop was going down. He glanced at his watch and realized Houston's shift ended in an hour. Yes, he agreed, they didn't have much time.

After hanging up the phone, Dales stepped out of his office, strode purposefully to the glassed cubicle where the dispatchers sat before their equipment, and inquired where Constable Sarah Houston was.

He had to wait a moment as the two dispatchers grappled with the heavy radio traffic.

"She's at PC Mercer's home, attending the attempted suicide," said one, anxious to get back to her work.

Dales's jaw dropped, heat rising up his throat and settling in his ears. "Mercer tried to kill himself?" He summoned what he could of his authoritative air, trying desperately to sound in control, even though he felt sick to his stomach.

The dispatcher nodded. "Gunshot wound to the head. Call came in about ten minutes ago."

Dales dashed from the cubicle and scooped a set of keys from the Peg Board.

His unmarked cruiser joined the jumble of police cars, their roof lights swirling a red glow around Kent Mercer's neighborhood. An ambulance, lights and siren activated, sped away as Dales rushed into the house, joining Sergeant Edgar and three other officers speaking in hushed tones in the kitchen.

Dales broke into the circle, demanding all the details as he anxiously glanced about for the rookie woman constable who had become his nemesis.

"Where's Houston?" he barked hoarsely, sweat popping out on his forehead.

"She just left in the ambulance with Mercer," Sergeant Edgar answered.

"Shit," Dales muttered, glancing at his watch again.

CHAPTER FOURTEEN

Stevie leaned close to Kent Mercer, keeping her knees firmly planted on the floor as the box of the ambulance swayed. She hated riding in a these damned things — it was like bobbing in a boat on turbulent water.

She strained to hear Mercer's words, occasionally pulling the oxygen mask away from his face as he spoke. It might be his last chance to come clean, she'd convinced him; he had nothing to lose now.

Yes, he admitted weakly, he'd known long ago about the parties, about the compromising positions some of his fellow officers were in. He'd never gone to the parties himself, had never been compromised.

"Why did Alsop want you guys in his pocket?" Stevie demanded breathlessly, knowing that at any moment Mercer might lose consciousness.

He struggled for breath again, fighting shock from the blood loss. "We had to . . . to turn a blind eye."

"To what?"

"The booze shipments he smuggled . . . from the border."

Stevie held on as the ambulance hit a bump. "Did you know they faked your fingerprints and planted them at Gina Walters's house and in Harding Scott's car?"

Mercer nodded wanly, his face as blanched as a peeled apple.

"Then why didn't you come forward?" she yelled over the screeching of the siren.

Mercer closed his eyes, opened them partway again. "Nobody would . . . have believed me. I didn't want to end up . . . like the other two. Just yesterday . . . they told me, one way or another . . . I was a dead man," he gasped.

Stevie nodded somberly. "So you were going to do it yourself instead of giving them the satisfaction. How did you get involved in all this?"

"I'd heard . . . about the parties. After my wife . . . was with Gina . . . the guys razzed me so bad, I threatened to tell their wives about the parties."

Stevie nodded, grasping the picture being painted for her. "So they compromised you by telling you about the smuggling, getting you involved in their scheme. And by planting your fingerprints, you had to keep quiet or they'd see that you were done for murder."

Mercer's eyelids fluttered one final time as he slipped into unconsciousness, the ambulance braking to an abrupt halt at the hospital emergency entrance.

Stevie helped the ambulance attendants unload the stretcher, watching with a mixture of worry and relief as hospital staff took over. They needed Mercer to live; they needed his testimony. But at least she had more pieces of the puzzle. They had enough now to get a warrant to search Alsop's property.

Stevie helped herself to a telephone at the nursing station, giving Jovanowski a brief rundown of what had happened, and told him where she had Kelly Bronskill hidden. He was on his way, he said, just give him a couple of hours to get there.

She couldn't go home. Alsop and his thugs might be looking for her there if they'd figured out she'd taken off with Kelly Bronskill, or that she'd had a conversation with Mercer. She'd finish out the thirty minutes left in her shift, kill some time in a public place, then meet Jovanowski at the dilapidated motel where Bronskill was stashed away.

Chief Bob Dales rushed up to the nursing station, tapping Stevie impatiently on the shoulder just as she'd put the phone down. Breathless from dashing through the hospital, he told her an alarm call had just come through at 1120 Greensway Lane, and he needed her to attend.

Stevie's eyebrows knotted in unwelcome surprise. Dales gave no sign that he recognized it as Bradley Alsop's address.

"I didn't hear the call," Stevie replied, indicating her portable two-way radio, which had been silent.

"Signals won't reach inside this place. The cement walls are too thick. Take my unmarked outside," he ordered, tossing her the keys.

"Backup?" Stevie inquired, a sense of dread balling in her stomach. She tried to ignore her fear that this was some kind of setup. She couldn't afford to panic, not when they were this close.

"As soon as someone's available, we'll send them. Edgar and Gardner were just sent to an assault in progress, and Jackson's at the scene of an accident."

Stevie frowned, wondering why Dales wasn't offering to join her since all the other officers on the shift were supposedly tied up.

As if reading her mind, Dales smiled apologetically. "Just routine. Alarms at this place all the time, it's so wired up. A cat will trip it, for crissakes. I'd go with you, but someone should stay here with Mercer."

Stevie felt nauseous, fairly certain now she was being set up, but she wouldn't — couldn't — show Dales her fear. She'd just have to be careful, radio in again for backup and wait outside Alsop's entrance. No way was she going inside those gates by herself.

Stevie retrieved a Kevlar vest from the trunk of the car, and thought of Mercer as she clicked her seat belt around her. Surely Dales wouldn't try to do something to him in the hospital. Nah, hurting him would be too obvious, and besides, Mercer would have to be taken into surgery soon. They wouldn't be letting anyone near him for a while.

Stevie pulled up to the gate of Bradley Alsop's estate, noting with annoyance that the place was shrouded in darkness. There were no outside lights on. She radioed in her location, asking again when backup would arrive.

It would be a few minutes, the dispatcher told her. The assault was a serious one, and there were injuries in the car accident.

Stevie rolled the window down an inch and turned the ignition off. She could hear a voice, low and faint. It sounded like a moan. She rolled the window down farther, straining to listen.

"Help," the voice, a man's, pleaded weakly from somewhere in the dark. Help me."

Haltingly, Stevie opened her door, her hand on the grip of her pistol. "Shit," she cursed out loud. She knew she shouldn't get out of the car, but what if it was legitimate? Maybe it wasn't a setup, she tried to reassure herself. There was no indication anyone knew she'd spirited Kelly Bronskill away, or that Mercer had told her everything. And besides, she wouldn't actually enter the grounds. She'd just try to get close enough to the gate to determine where the voice was coming from. She was a cop, and ignoring a call for help just wasn't something she could bring herself to do.

Staying low on the driveway, still on the street side of the gate, she crept a few feet in the direction of the voice, the moaning continuing. She drew her pistol. She'd take no chances this was just some injured bystander.

The crack of the first shot froze her in place, numbed her mind; everything slowed to freeze-frame, as though she were watching herself in a movie. She'd never been under live fire before, and, still in denial, wondered curiously if gunfire was really what she'd heard. *Maybe it's just a car backfir —*

The second and third shots popped, sounding like firecrackers, shattering Stevie's idle thoughts. No doubt about it. This was war.

A bullet whined over her head. Suddenly, Stevie's thoughts ignited, adrenaline thawing her inaction. She told herself to breathe evenly. She looked around, took stock of her surroundings. Knowing she was a sitting duck, she quickly scampered in front of a waist-high brick pillar supporting the iron fencing, fairly certain the shooter was almost directly across from her now, somewhere on Alsop's property. She'd have made for the car, but it was farther away than the pillar, and crossing through the line of fire was suicidal.

Stevie shouted into her portable radio. "Shots fired. Officer needs assistance."

She couldn't hear the response over more gunfire. Could even be an automatic weapon, she told herself, still clutching her police-issue .40-caliber semi-automatic pistol. Calmly, she mentally calculated her own firepower. She had a total of thirty-seven rounds on her, plus her Beretta strapped to her ankle and its seven rounds.

A shot whizzed past Stevie's ear, paralyzingly close. The gunman had moved, getting a better angle on her. Dropping to her belly, Stevie crawled to the other pillar, cursing under her breath, praying that backup would arrive soon, and that she would just get the hell out of this in one piece. She rose up slightly, just to take a peek at the flash of gunfire to see where the bastard was. If only she could get a line on him —

Like a ferocious kick, something pounded Stevie in the back, spinning her halfway around and slamming her to the ground, shoulder first. Only after she hit the ground did she hear the crack of gunfire, and it confused her, muddied her thoughts again. *I can't be shot,* she futilely consoled self, panic edging ever closer. *I would have heard the shot before I felt it, dammit.*

She dragged herself up to a crouching position, wincing and cursing through clenched teeth, her left shoulder throbbing like hell. She pulled her right hand up and fired back. She emptied her clip in the direction of the shots, painfully jammed a fresh clip in and blasted away again, the shots perfectly cadenced as though she were on a target range. What the hell, she figured, as her gun blasted for all it was worth. She was hemmed in; there was nowhere else to go. If they wanted to get her, they'd get her, but she'd at least go down fighting.

Stevie reloaded and waited for the return of fire, but there was none. Her trembling legs could no longer support her. With a muffled thud, she crashed backward to the snow-packed ground, the gun still in her grip.

"Christ," she whispered desperately to the darkness, her teeth clamped against the excruciating pain in her shoulder. When she tried to move, it jolted her in evil mockery, keeping her pinned. She turned her head, wincing, and it was then she saw the bloody patch of snow spreading out beneath her.

Oh Jade! she cried out in her mind, tears stinging her eyes, her breath caught in her constricted throat. She was suddenly scared shitless of never seeing her lover again — that she'd die right here, in the snow, in the dark, all alone, some goddamned one-minute hero. *I'm sorry, Jade, I'm so sorry I fucked up.* God, how she wanted to live, even just long enough to see Jade again, to tell her how much she loved her, to tell her how sorry she was for letting this happen, for hurting her.

Her mind began to spin along with the red roof lights of an approaching police car, its siren piercing her garbled thoughts, ringing in her ears. The cold fingers of her free hand clawed at the snow. She could almost feel the silkiness of Jade's hair, could faintly smell the sweet shampoo . . .

Stevie mumbled Jade's name over and over as Sue Jackson cradled her head, having already placed her coat over the shivering Stevie.

She couldn't grasp the consoling words Jackson was mumbling to her, didn't want to. She only wanted Jade's soothing voice, her soft, capable hands, her reassuring smile.

CHAPTER FIFTEEN

So sedated was Stevie for the first twenty-four hours, she was mercifully unaware of the chaotic activity around her — the X rays and MRI, the emergency surgery to repair her shredded shoulder, the worried bedside vigils, the property searches and arrests made by Jovanowski and his team of government helpers.

When her awareness began to seep back into her like water trickling from a leaky faucet, it was Jade's face she recognized, staring worriedly at her and holding her hand. Jade must have noticed the drugged haziness ebbing from Stevie's eyes, because a smile formed across her fatigued face, and she closed her eyes for a moment, either in silent prayer or relief, Stevie wasn't sure.

Stevie watched the heavy intake of breath and saw where worry had etched itself around Jade's eyes, in the corners of her pinched mouth.

"Stevie, you . . ." The words came out choked, and Jade could go no further.

Stevie tried to smile. "I know, Jade, I know," she replied weakly.

Stevie knew what would come once she got home. There would be a couple of days of denial, of pretend emotional apathy. Then the tears would come, and they'd have a couple of arguments about Stevie's job and its risks. Then a day or two later, Jade would calm down, would reluctantly admit Stevie wouldn't be half the woman she was if she couldn't be a cop. That said, they'd make love, the most tender, most nurturing of lovemaking, and it'd be like really coming home.

"I want to go home," Stevie mumbled, her eyes brimming, a small smile at the corners of her parched lips.

Jade grinned, still clutching Stevie's hand. She winked. "Only if we can get all these flowers in the house."

Stevie glanced around, grimacing in pain as she moved her head. The trauma had left her whole body sore. "Who are all these from?"

"From the police department, one from Jocelyn Travers, one from Dana Jeffries, and one from Sue Jackson." Jade winked. "Should I be jealous of all these women sending you flowers?"

Stevie smiled. "What does Dana's card say?"

Jade stood, went to a vase of crisp yellow roses, and pinched the card between her fingers. "It says: 'To Stevie. Hope you will be back on the job soon, especially now that I'm living in your city. I can't thank you enough for all you've done. Dana.' "

Stevie smiled. "I'm so glad she didn't have anything to do with the murders."

"The newspapers love you too," Jade bubbled. "You should see —"

"Tex, you're awake!" Jovanowski almost ran into the room, a huge grin on his wide face, a bouquet of limp carnations in his hand.

"Isn't it wonderful?" Jade beamed, taking the flowers from him.

Jovanowski sat down on the edge of the bed as gently as his hulking frame would allow, then bashfully kissed Stevie's hand. "You're gonna be okay. The doc says you'll need a couple of months of physio once it heals up, but you'll be as good as new. She says there's no permanent nerve damage."

Stevie nodded grimly at the thought of the weeks of recuperation ahead of her. "What the hell happened anyway? I hardly even remember being hit."

Jovanowski exhaled slowly. "You were damn lucky, Tex. The ammo went right through your body armor, but luckily only ripped up muscle and soft tissue. And it was just dumb luck that you got him, all dressed in black the way he was. He was using a semiautomatic rifle. It was only a matter of time if you hadn't got him."

Jade went to the window, turning her back on them. It was difficult for her to hear what Stevie had been through and even more difficult to fathom what could have happened. She knew the dangers of Stevie's job, had known them all along. She understood the excitement and exhilaration Stevie felt when she started putting the pieces of a case together, when it was time to make an arrest. Jade shared those same feelings every time she carved up a corpse and unraveled the cause of death. But at least her subjects were all dead. Stevie's, on the other hand, were very much alive and very dangerous.

Stevie swallowed, her throat dry from the tubes that had earlier been there. "It was a setup, wasn't it," she whispered hoarsely.

Jovanowski nodded. "Tried to make it look like an intruder who panicked at seeing a cop there and fired. It was some drip named Mancuso. He was on Alsop's payroll."

"Was?"

Jovanowski nodded gravely again, unsure of what to say to Stevie as she turned her head slightly into the pillow. He had been on the force almost three times as long as Stevie, but he had never killed anyone.

He patted her good shoulder and continued. "We searched Alsop's warehouses."

"And?" Stevie asked, perking up.

Jovanowski smiled appreciatively. "You were right about everything. Alsop was smuggling booze over the border in hollowed-out computer hard drives and monitors. In fact he had a whole tractor-trailer load at his warehouse — about $350,000 worth of rye whiskey."

"He was distributing it too?"

"We've brought the Mounties in on it since border

smuggling is their specialty. But they tell me the way it usually works is that the shipment comes into the warehouse, but doesn't stay long. It's loaded onto smaller trucks, usually about fifty cases apiece, and goes directly to taverns and restaurants." Jovanowski shrugged. "It's cut-rate. Hard to turn down cheap booze, and the RCMP says it's not hard to find buyers."

"Have you got Alsop in custody?"

Jovanowski grinned. "Caught him trying to cross the border last night. Got Dales too, and he's already admitted everything. Cracked like a cheap piece of china."

"So he was in on it from the start?" Stevie asked, disgusted.

"Got a little piece of the profits for keeping his men out of Alsop's hair — that and the videos showing these guys in compromising positions. We've made a few arrests already, and there'll be plenty more once the net widens."

Jovanowski's mouth curled down in contempt. "Guess who else had his fingers in the pie? Jim Scott."

Stevie shook her head slowly. "I knew I didn't like that guy. Jesus. What was his role?"

"He was one of a handful of computer store owners Alsop pretended he was supplying with his phony computers."

"But his own dad, for crissakes. Did he know his dad was investigating this?"

Jovanowski shook his head. "Not until after his dad's death. There's no evidence he had anything to do with Gina's death or his dad's. It's bad enough he was on Alsop's payroll, and he must have felt damn guilty about it. He admitted he was the anonymous tipster Jocelyn told us about."

Stevie frowned. "Don't tell me he was one of the playboys on Alsop's home videos. Is that how he got into all this?"

Jovanowski nodded. "Yep, 'fraid so. He's being extremely cooperative with us, though. That's why he finally brought us his dad's safety-deposit box stuff. Guess he finally figured his anonymous calls weren't going anywhere. Amazing what guilt can do to a person."

"What about Kent Mercer?"

"It'll take a while to get all the evidence gathered, but with his testimony, and Kelly Bronskill's, and others once they come out of the woodwork, it'll be pretty airtight."

"Is Mercer okay?"

Jovanowski shifted his weight on the bed. "Fortunately, the bullet didn't do a lot of damage — ricocheted off a bone and out his ear. He wasn't using hollow points, just full metal. We're putting him into a pretty strict counseling program. That boy needs a lot of help; he's got a lot of guilt."

"And what's going to happen to Kelly?"

Jovanowski's eyebrows lifted hopefully. "She's agreed to come to Toronto and enroll in a special program for hookers who want to get off the street — after she goes through a rehab program, of course."

Stevie smiled, feeling like it was the only positive thing to come out of the case. "I'm glad. I hope she makes it."

Her thoughts turned to Gina Walters and Harding Scott. She felt a gnawing emptiness inside, a void where once she had felt so much pride for the uniform, for being a cop. But cops had killed these two cops. Even if it was Alsop's thugs who had actually pulled the trigger, the cops who had crossed the line of the law to satiate their greed had contributed to their murders just as much.

Stevie stared up at the sterile ceiling tiles as if silently counting them. The law was sometimes a narrow line, and she knew there was always temptation for a cop to cross that line, whether it was taking a cut of drug money, pocketing confiscated property, or beating the living crap out of someone for the sheer power of it. But once a cop crossed that line, he or she was forever compromised, the badge irrevocably tarnished.

She knew now what Gina Walters had been talking about in her diary, how, after breaking this case, she didn't know if she could give her heart to policing again. Stevie felt the same heaviness of heart.

Reading the despair on her face, Jovanowski squeezed her hand. "Listen to me, Stevie. These guys will be put away for a long time; they'll never wear a uniform again. And you showed this town and everybody out there that there are good cops, cops who will do whatever it takes to uphold the law."

Stevie shook her head lightly, rage pulsing through her. "But these guys ... they're animals, Ted. For the first time in my career, I don't feel any pleasure in putting away a criminal. They make me too sick to feel any satisfaction."

Jade joined them, her fingers gently caressing Stevie's head. "But you're a hero, hon. You should be proud of that."

Jovanowski smiled. "You should hear McLemore

raving about what a wonder cop you are. He's putting you in for a commendation, says he's going to submit your name to the governor-general's office for a Medal of Bravery."

Stevie laughed. "From the doghouse to Parliament Hill. Quite a climb up in just a few months time."

Jovanowski grinned. "Damn right. And I'm going to be right there on your coattails. You're my shooting star."

"You mean I'm your ticket to avoiding early retirement."

"Shit, yes. I'm not ready to sit at home and twiddle my thumbs yet."

Jade touched his shoulder, mischief in her eyes. "Maybe it wouldn't be so bad if you had someone waiting at home for you. And I could probably think of someone."

A red tide roared up Jovanowski's neck, settling in his face. "You two stay out of that, you hear? I don't need you fixing me up with Jocelyn Travers. I'm quite capable of handling my own love life."

"Did I hear my name?" Jocelyn Travers entered the room with yet another bouquet of flowers.

Jade, Jovanowski, and Stevie glanced furtively at one another before erupting into muffled giggles.

Jocelyn set the flowers down and gently squeezed both of Stevie's hands, smiling widely, relief twinkling in her blue eyes. "I'm so glad you're going to be OK."

Stevie smiled back. "You're not the only one." She introduced Jade, who was again caressing Stevie's head. There was no need to explain their relationship.

"Jade's my favorite doc," Jovanowski added.

Jocelyn's smile was one of approval as she appraised Stevie and Jade. "I can see you're very lucky, Stevie. And having a doctor around while you recuperate won't hurt either."

Stevie, Jade, and Jovanowski burst into laughter, a little too heartily as the stress of the last twenty-four hours receded. Finally, Jovanowski felt the need to explain the inside joke to Jocelyn.

"She's not that kind of doc, actually. She's a forensic pathologist."

Jocelyn laughed, her face pinking, and moved behind Jovanowski. "Let's hope you don't need those services."

Stevie shifted carefully to make herself more comfortable, Jade helping her like a mother hen.

"Listen, Jocelyn," Stevie said, subduing a smile. "Life's pretty damn short, you know. And if Ted won't tell you, then I will."

Jovanowski's jaw dropped. His eyes registered fear of what was next.

Stevie plowed on. "Ted here has a huge crush on you and he wants to ask you out for a date."

Jovanowski coughed and sputtered, then stood up as though he might make a break for it. He shot Stevie an I'm-going-to-kill-you glare.

"Is that true?" Jocelyn looked at Jovanowski.

Jovanowski shrugged, his face as red as a freshly painted barn. "Well, y-yes," he stammered. "I would, you know, like to ask you out some time."

Jocelyn smiled. "Sounds like a good idea to me."

EPILOGUE

"You know, honey," Jade smiled sweetly, her voice delicate. "I was really lonely here while you were away. And I was thinking, you know, about maybe expanding our little family."

Stevie clutched her coffee cup tightly, her knuckles whitening. Sweat gathered in tiny rivulets under her arms and slithered down her sides, dampening her bathrobe. Her shoulder ached again. The throbbing always became worse when she was worried about something.

"What's wrong, Stevie? You look like you've just seen a ghost or something." Jade's smile turned inquisitive.

Stevie swallowed, looked expectantly at the ceiling for inspiration but finding none. Christ, could Jade be serious? *Expanding our family?*

When she finally spoke, she kept her voice subdued and even, not wanting to upset Jade before they'd had a chance to at least talk it calmly through. But, a baby? *Jesus, God.* Stevie shook her head despondently. She wasn't ready for this, might never be.

"Honey, I know you're thirty-seven years old and you don't have much time left, but —"

"What?" Jade exclaimed, her forehead wrinkling in confusion. "What do you mean, you think I'm going to die tomorrow or something?"

Stevie looked at Jade, her eyebrows poised. Jade wasn't going to make this one easy on her. "Honey" Stevie reached for Jade's hand, stroked it soothingly. "I understand you feeling the need to have a baby, I really do, but — "

"A baby?" A look of surprise, then horror swept Jade's face. Then she laughed, straight from the belly, her body shaking with hysteria.

Stevie froze, perplexed, her heart still stuttering. She didn't dare laugh along with Jade — not yet, anyway.

Finally, Jade's laughter subsided long enough for her to speak, tears dotting the corners of her eyes. "Oh, honey, you think I'm talking about a baby?" Jade fell into another fit of laughter.

Irritated, Stevie snapped back. "Well, what else am I supposed to think when you sit there, all serious, and say you want to 'expand our family'?"

Jade leaned over the table and kissed her. "You are so cute, Stephanie Elizabeth Houston."

Stevie rolled her eyes. "So we're not having a baby?"

Jade shook her head, traces of amusement still lighting her face. "No, I don't want a baby — at least not in the foreseeable future."

Stevie exhaled in relief, collapsing forward. "Oh, thank god."

"But yes, I am talking about expanding our family. Just a minute."

Jade dashed off, leaving Stevie with her cooling coffee. It was minutes before she noisily clanged her way into the house, the cool April air following her in. Stevie could hear scurrying, scratching noises on what sounded like tin. She got up to investigate but sat back down as Jade yelled at her to stay where she was, her shoulder throbbing its thanks.

It was another minute before Jade came into the sunny kitchen, her jacket over the squirming lump in her arms.

"What the hell are you doing?" Stevie asked curiously, not enjoying all the secrecy.

Jade's smile was as wide as a canyon. She slipped the jacket off, letting it drop to the floor.

Stevie's mouth fell open as Jade came closer with the fluffy, chubby little ball of yellow fur.

"A dog? You went and got us a dog? Jesus, Jade, you could have talked to me about it first."

"Oh, c'mon you old grump. If I had, you would have just said no."

Stevie pouted at the accusation. "I like dogs," she answered defensively. "But it's going to tie us down, and what about the long hours we put in at work?"

The puppy whined contentedly, suckling on Jade's finger. "We'll work it out, and besides, you're off work for another month. Just think, it'll be all housetrained by then."

Stevie grimaced, shaking her head. "Great, I get to sit at home for a month looking after a goddamned misbehaved, untrained puppy."

"Well, it beats fooling around on the Internet all day, which I know you've been doing." Jade winked.

"I do not fool around on the Internet all day. And besides, even if I did, I don't think a puppy beats the peace and quiet of the computer."

Jade plopped the wriggling ball onto Stevie's lap. "Stevie, this is Taffy. Taffy, this is your other mommie, Stevie."

Stevie fumbled with it, checked under its belly. "I see you at least picked a female. That's good. What the hell kind of mutt is this thing, anyway?"

Jade reached down to pet it. "She's a golden retriever. She should grow to about seventy pounds. They're good dogs, Stevie. And she'll be company for us when one of us is working late. I'll feel better about having a dog around."

The pup nuzzled Stevie's neck, then happily licked her chin.

A smile slowly broke Stevie's surliness. "All right, all right. Let's keep her. But we're not calling her some wimpy little name like Taffy!"

Jade beamed, kissing each of them in turn. "Our little family is complete now. But what would you suggest calling her?"

Stevie thought for a moment. "Counterfeit."

"Forget it, we're not calling her after something illegal."

"Okay, how about Winchester?"

"After a gun? Oh, that's brilliant." Jade, hands on her hips, studied the pup, then proclaimed triumphantly, "Tonka! Is that sufficiently butch for you?"

Stevie nodded approvingly before her face suddenly soured. She quickly handed Tonka to Jade. A wet patch was spreading on her robed thigh, and Jade laughed as Stevie rolled her eyes.

"Welcome to parenthood, Stevie."

A few of the publications of
THE NAIAD PRESS, INC.
P.O. Box 10543   Tallahassee, Florida 32302
Phone (850) 539-5965
Toll-Free Order Number: 1-800-533-1973
Web Site: WWW.NAIADPRESS.COM
Mail orders welcome. Please include 15% postage.
Write or call for our free catalog which also features an
incredible selection of lesbian videos.

OVER THE LINE by Tracey Richardson. 176 pp. 2nd Stevie
Houston mystery.   ISBN 1-56280-202-X $11.95

JULIA'S SONG by Ann O'Leary. 208 pp. Strangely
disturbing . . . strangely exciting.   ISBN 1-56280-197-X   11.95

LOVE IN THE BALANCE by Marianne K. Martin. 256 pp.
Weighing the costs of love . . .   ISBN 1-56280-199-6   11.95

PIECE OF MY HEART by Julia Watts. 208 pp. All the
stuff that dreams are made of —   ISBN 1-56280-206-2   11.95

MAKING UP FOR LOST TIME by Karin Kallmaker. 240 pp.
Nobody does it better . . .   ISBN 1-56280-196-1   11.95

GOLD FEVER by Lyn Denison. 224 pp. By author of *Dream
Lover.*   ISBN 1-56280-201-1   11.95

WHEN THE DEAD SPEAK by Therese Szymanski. 224 pp. 2nd
Brett Higgins mystery.   ISBN 1-56280-198-8   11.95

FOURTH DOWN by Kate Calloway. 240 pp. 4th Cassidy James
mystery.   ISBN 1-56280-205-4   11.95

A MOMENT'S INDISCRETION by Peggy J. Herring. 176 pp.
There's a fine line between love and lust . . .   ISBN 1-56280-194-5   11.95

CITY LIGHTS/COUNTRY CANDLES by Penny Hayes. 208 pp.
About the women she has known . . .   ISBN 1-56280-195-3   11.95

POSSESSIONS by Kaye Davis. 240 pp. 2nd Maris Middleton
mystery.   ISBN 1-56280-192-9   11.95

A QUESTION OF LOVE by Saxon Bennett. 208 pp. Every
woman is granted one great love.   ISBN 1-56280-205-4   11.95

RHYTHM TIDE by Frankie J. Jones. 160 pp. . . . to desire
passionately and be passionately desired.   ISBN 1-56280-189-9   11.95

PENN VALLEY PHOENIX by Janet McClellan. 208 pp. 2nd
Tru North Mystery.   ISBN 1-56280-200-3   11.95

BY RESERVATION ONLY by Jackie Calhoun. 240 pp. A
chance for true happiness.   ISBN 1-56280-191-0   11.95

OLD BLACK MAGIC by Jaye Maiman. 272 pp. 9th Robin
Miller mystery.   ISBN 1-56280-175-9   11.95

LEGACY OF LOVE by Marianne K. Martin. 240 pp. Women
will do anything for her . . .   ISBN 1-56280-184-8   11.95

LETTING GO by Ann O Leary. 160 pp. Laura, at 39, in love
with 23-year-old Kate.   ISBN 1-56280-183-X   11.95

LADY BE GOOD edited by Barbara Grier and Christine Cassidy.
288 pp. Erotic stories by Naiad Press authors. ISBN 1-56280-180-5   14.95

CHAIN LETTER by Claire McNab. 288 pp. 9th Carol Ashton
mystery.   ISBN 1-56280-181-3   11.95

NIGHT VISION by Laura Adams. 256 pp. Erotic fantasy romance
by "famous" author.   ISBN 1-56280-182-1   11.95

SEA TO SHINING SEA by Lisa Shapiro. 256 pp. Unable to resist
the raging passion . . .   ISBN 1-56280-177-5   11.95

THIRD DEGREE by Kate Calloway. 224 pp. 3rd Cassidy James
mystery.   ISBN 1-56280-185-6   11.95

WHEN THE DANCING STOPS by Therese Szymanski. 272 pp.
1st Brett Higgins mystery.   ISBN 1-56280-186-4   11.95

PHASES OF THE MOON by Julia Watts. 192 pp. . . . . . hungry
for everything life has to offer.   ISBN 1-56280-176-7   11.95

BABY IT'S COLD by Jaye Maiman. 256 pp. 5th Robin Miller
mystery.   ISBN 1-56280-156-2   10.95

CLASS REUNION by Linda Hill. 176 pp. The girl from her past . . .
                                              ISBN 1-56280-178-3   11.95

DREAM LOVER by Lyn Denison. 224 pp. A soft, sensuous,
romantic fantasy.   ISBN 1-56280-173-1   11.95

FORTY LOVE by Diana Simmonds. 288 pp. Joyous, heart-
warming romance.   ISBN 1-56280-171-6   11.95

IN THE MOOD by Robbi Sommers. 160 pp. The queen of
erotic tension!   ISBN 1-56280-172-4   11.95

SWIMMING CAT COVE by Lauren Douglas. 192 pp. 2nd
Allison O Neil Mystery.   ISBN 1-56280-168-6   11.95

These are just a few of the many Naiad Press titles — we are the oldest and
largest lesbian/feminist publishing company in the world. We also offer an
enormous selection of lesbian video products. Please request a complete
catalog. We offer personal service; we encourage and welcome direct mail
orders from individuals who have limited access to bookstores carrying our
publications.